D0340315

QUINNY & HOPPER

Smart Cookies

Written by Adriana Brad Schanen

Illustrated by Charles Santoso

DISNEY • HYPERION

Los Angeles • New York

First Edition, June 2018
10 9 8 7 6 5 4 3 2 1
FAC-020093-18110
Printed in the United States of America

This book is set in Century Schoolbook Std, Weber Hand ITC Std,
Arial Narrow MT Pro/Monotype; Typography of Coop/House Industries;
Myriad Std Tilt, Billy Serif/Fontspring
Designed by Tyler Nevins

Library of Congress Cataloging-in-Publication Data
Names: Schanen, Adriana Brad. • Santoso, Charles, illustrator.
Title: Smart cookies / by Adriana Brad Schanen ; illustrated
by Charles Santoso.
Description: First edition. • Los Angeles ; New York :
Disney-Hyperion, 2018. • Series: [Quinny & Hopper ; 3] • Summary:
"Quinny petitions to overturn a new school-wide
ban on sweets, Hopper reinvents the 'Friendship Bench' at
recess, and both learn to embrace the qualities that make
them who they are"— Provided by publisher.
Identifiers: LCCN 2017056153 • ISBN 9781368019033 (hardback)
Subjects: • CYAC: Best friends—Fiction. • Friendship—Fiction. •
Individuality—Fiction. • Schools—Fiction. • Humorous stories. •
BISAC: JUVENILE FICTION / Social Issues / Friendship. • JUVENILE
FICTION / Humorous Stories. • JUVENILE
FICTION / School & Education.
Classification: LCC PZ7.S33376 Sm 2018 • DDC [Fic]—dc23
LC record available at https://lccn.loc.gov/2017056153

Reinforced binding

Visit www.DisneyBooks.com

For the passionate educators and young
readers at Charles H. Bullock School—
a great place to be a kid.

And for my extraordinary niece,
Lauren Beloff, a fourth-grade teacher who
changes lives every day.

One

Quinny

I can't believe Daddy's arguing with a baby. And that baby—my sister, Cleo—is winning.

"Drop it," he orders. "Sweetie, you're a big girl, spit it out."

Cleo's strong eyes stare up at Daddy and her strong mouth does NOT let that Binky go. "Mrrrrrfff," she growls.

"Where did she even find that thing?" says Mom. "I thought you hid them all."

"I thought I did, too," says Daddy.

Mom makes a stressed-out smile, and Piper, my monkey sister, sits in her underpants (her usual breakfast outfit) eating a banana plus saltines (her usual breakfast food) and I'm slurping my cereal and trying to think of some helpful advice, because Daddy can't handle this interesting Monday morning we're having. He can't convince Piper to put clothes on even though it's November, or finish her homework sheets (homework in kindergarten—who invented that?). He can't make Cleo give up her Binky. And it's all driving him slightly coconuts.

"Put some plain yogurt on the Binky," I suggest. There's nothing Cleo hates more than the tart-sour taste of Mom's favorite breakfast.

"Promise her a tree house," says Piper, who really wants a tree house.

"Dip it in cayenne pepper," says Mom.

"Didn't we try that last week?" says Daddy.

"No, that was garlic powder," says Mom.

My parents are trying to make Cleo give up her Binky because our pediatrician told them to, or her teeth might not grow in right. Plus, Mom doesn't think a person who is almost two years old should need to suck on a plastic blob to feel okay about life. (At least not during the day. At night, my parents are still afraid of Cleo, who is the world's worst sleeper, so they give her that Binky and put LOTS of extras in her crib. My baby sister sleeps in a forest of Binkies.)

While Daddy and Cleo play tug-of-war with her Binky, I walk to our dining nook—it's not big enough to be called a *room*—to feed my guinea pig and fill his water tube. That's my only animal-care job these days, since my neighbor Mrs. Porridge's chicken coop is down to just one hen, named Cha-Cha, who mostly eats cat food with Mrs. Porridge's cat, named Walter. We've been begging Mrs. Porridge to get more chickens, but she said not to hold our breath.

"Good morning, Crescent!" I call out, on my way to his cage.

Usually he answers me with some happy squeaking, but today there's just silence.

"Crescent?"

I named my soft, warm, roly-poly guinea pig after my favorite soft, warm, roly-poly bread rolls. His cage used to be in my room, but he got too noisy at night, so we moved him down to our dining nook, where we never eat since the table is usually covered in laundry that Daddy hasn't folded, homework we haven't done, and messy paper-piles of I don't even know what.

"Crescent? Good morning, cutie, where are you?"

I look all around his cage, in his little playhouse, and by the cozy corner under his food dish. Then I notice the door to his cage is unlatched, and a tiny bit open.

"Oh no, Mom—Crescent is gone!!!" I zoom back to the kitchen. "Piper, what did you do!!! Where's Crescent!"

Nearly naked Piper runs away and leaps up the stairs, two at a time—which means she's guilty of something.

"Get back here! Mom, help! Daddy, Piper opened the cage and Crescent's gone!"

"Honey, calm down." Mom is by my side now, but I can barely breathe.

"Where is he? We have to find him or Walter will eat him up!"

Walter hangs out in our yard sometimes and likes to kill birds. (But not all birds—his best friend and sidekick is Cha-Cha the chicken, who rides around on his back.)

Mom and I look for Crescent everywhere—in the cupboards, closet, oven, and trash can. In all the backpacks. In the giant, grubby pile of shoes by our kitchen door.

"Mom! Wait—I saw something move! Over there!"

"Where?"

"There, between the muddy Croc and that old sneaker!"

Mom grabs one of Piper's dusty sneakers from the pile of shoes and flips it upside down. A greenish baby carrot and a dust ball fall out, but no Crescent.

"Nice," says Mom, giving Daddy a look. "Do these even still fit her anymore?"

Mom and Daddy start arguing now about the mountain of shoes. She drives to her job, but he works in an office right in our upstairs hall closet, so Mom says he's the one who should keep everything "organized and under control" at home. But then Daddy blames all the messy shoes on me, and says I should help clean more, since I'm the oldest kid. But hey, I never asked to be the oldest kid! (I did ask to be the *only* kid, but nobody listened.)

My parents are so busy arguing that they're not even helping me look for Crescent.

Piper comes back downstairs and we look in every shoe. Even the really smelly ones.

"There he is!" cries Piper. "Get him!"

Crescent's beady little eye peeks out from behind a tall rubber rain boot, and his mouth nibbles on an old crust of bread. I leap toward that rubber boot, but he disappears.

I am excellent at catching chickens, but not so great at catching guinea pigs, I guess.

And then I hear a familiar roar coming from down the street. Uh-oh. That's the bus headed to Whisper Valley Elementary School. Mom says *hurry-we-can-still-make-it-if-we-run.*

"But Mom, I can't go to school when my precious Crescent is missing."

"You have no choice, Quinny—I've got an early meeting. Daddy will keep looking—"

But then, as Mom opens the back door to drag us outside, Crescent jumps down from a potted plant on the windowsill and scurries out, too, right in between Piper's ankles.

"Crescent, stop!!! Piper, watch out!!" I run after that sneaky guinea pig and lunge for him, but I just get kicked in the nose by Piper's confused feet.

KONK!

Piper falls on me and starts crying. Then Cleo comes and sits on me and starts crying, too, through her Binky, because she doesn't like being left out of anything, not even tears. And Mom doesn't even punish Piper for kicking me in the face! She yells at *me*, and makes me keep running to the bus, even though my nose just got smashed and my guinea pig is definitely being eaten by Mrs. Porridge's awful cat right this very instant.

I've had some bad luck in my life, but this has got to be my bad-luckiest day ever.

Really, truly, absolutely.

Two

Hopper

The first bell rings and everyone's walking into class when I spot Quinny, rushing down the hall. Her nose is red, her watermelon barrette dangles from a knot in her hair, and she's dropping her stuff everywhere. I go and help her pick it up.

"Quinny, you weren't on the bus."

"Oh, Hopper, I already know that! We missed it by just a few tiny seconds."

"Are you okay?"

"Fantastic. Except Crescent ran away and Daddy was fighting with Cleo's Binky and I got blamed for the mountain of shoes and Piper didn't even get a consequence for kicking me in the

8

nose. By the way, have you seen Crescent? I think Walter ate him up for breakfast."

The second bell rings. That means we're supposed to be sitting at our desks already.

"Hopper, oh no! Mrs. Flavio is going to breathe fire at me if I'm late again, come on."

I follow Quinny, but she stops just before the classroom door. I almost crash into her.

"Wait, Hopper, tell the truth—do you think Crescent is still alive?" Her eyes look so worried. Her Cheerios breath comes out fast. "Or did Walter really eat him up in one big gulp?"

I want to tell Quinny that Crescent will be okay. But the truth is, I just don't know.

It takes me a moment to figure out what to say. I'm not very good at being hopeful.

"Don't worry, he's going to be fine," I finally tell her.

Quinny looks relieved. I just hope that being hopeful isn't a lie.

At recess, Quinny's usually one of the first people to burst out onto the field, but today I don't see her. Then I realize my left shoelaces are loose, so I stop to tie them, on a bench.

"What are you doing?"

I look up to see Kaitlin, one of Victoria's friends. Her hand is on her hip. Her glittery nail polish matches her glittery socks. Her sneakers are covered in cats.

"Um, tying my shoe?" I don't like it when my laces get all dirty.

"No, I mean . . ." Kaitlin gestures to some words that are drawn on the bench behind me:

Whisper Valley Elementary School
FRIENDSHIP BENCH.
Give some & get some, right here!

Oh. I didn't realize that's where I was sitting. I was absent for my tonsillectomy operation when they put this new bench on the playground last month. No one really uses it.

I'm about to get up. But Kaitlin sits down next to me and lets out a groan.

"Victoria thinks this is so dumb . . . the whole Friendship Bench thing," she says.

Kaitlin didn't ask a question, but it seems like she's waiting for an answer.

"Victoria is just one person," I say.

"I know, but I can't believe you're actually sitting here. No one sits here."

"I told you, I was just tying my shoe." I'm not looking for friends. I just want to go find Quinny. I see her across the playground, zooming down the slide with her mouth open so wide that a bird could fly into it. I hear her laugh. The sound of it makes my shoulders relax.

I start to get up, but Kaitlin says, "Wait. . . ." Her mouth twitches. She looks upset. "She thinks she's so smart. Victoria . . . but if people only knew . . ."

Knew what? She glares over at Victoria, who is Hula-Hooping with some girls. Victoria's not my favorite person. But she *is* smart. What's wrong with thinking you're smart if it's true?

"This fell out of Victoria's backpack." Kaitlin unfolds a tiny piece of paper in her fist.

SMART LIST

1) Victoria Porridge
2) Hopper Grey

3) Avery Bedoya

4) Caleb Demefack

5) Nidhi Gupta

6) Jayson Washington

7) Izzy Friedlich

8) Connor Rivington

9) Maeve Bradley

10) Alex Delgado

11) Xander Cross

12) Cassie Emmert

13) Jake Wu

14) Sawyer Lukowski

15) Kaitlin Kuperschmidt

16) McKayla Derring

17) Kailee Hollins

18) Cecily Kaufman

19) Buck Cressidy

20) TJ Shipley

21) Johnnie Hong

22) Juniper Dunne

23) Lydia Foster-Madsen

24) Quinny Bumble

The first thing I notice is the first name on

the list: Victoria's. The next thing I notice is the last name: Quinny's. In between are the names of everyone else in our class.

"Can you believe she would do that to Quinny?" says Kaitlin.

Actually, I can.

"Don't worry, nobody's going to believe Victoria's smarter than you," she says.

I don't care about that. This whole list is bad, no matter what number Victoria gave me.

"I'm pretty dumb, but hey, at least I'm not as dumb as Quinny." Kaitlin laughs.

"Stop it. You should rip that thing up," I tell her. "Quinny's not dumb. Neither are you."

Kaitlin snorts. "How would you know?"

I don't know why I'm still sitting here. I guess I feel bad for Kaitlin. She looks so glum.

"Why don't you ever play with Alex and Caleb and Xander?" she asks me.

I shrug. I do run around with them, sometimes.

"I mean, why do you always just sit here with a *book*?"

I sit on the stairs when I read at recess, not on this bench. But I don't correct Kaitlin.

"It's really good." I show her my book. "You can borrow it when I'm done."

Kaitlin's face puckers. "If you had Quinny all to yourself, you wouldn't have to sit here with your dumb book." Her breath falls out, rough and thick. Her words are mean, but sound sad.

I wish I could explain it, and make Kaitlin understand. Reading isn't something I do because I have no one to play with. I read because I want to know what it's like to jump out of an airplane. Because I want to play basketball at the Olympics, be a bear in the woods. Reading isn't something I do, it's somewhere I go. *Books don't have covers, they have doors.* My second-grade teacher, Ms. Rivers, said that last year. But Kaitlin wasn't in my class last year. Maybe her teacher never said that. And if I tell her now, she'll probably laugh and call me a dork.

But, fine—it's true. I'm a dork who likes sitting with a book. Playing loud games at recess isn't always fun for me. Quinny gets that. She and I are friends, even though we don't play together every single recess. I wish she were the one here with me now, not Kaitlin.

And then, I see that my wish is about to come true. Quinny's on her way over here.

She's running and smiling and waving at me. Her windy hair looks alive.

Right away I hide the Smart List behind my back.

I can't let her see it. I try to keep my face calm.

Maybe she won't even notice I'm holding anything.

Three

Quinny

School is the place where I have to sit still forever.

And sitting still is not easy, especially since Mrs. Flavio always glares at my wiggly hands and tappy feet. She's our long-term sub while Ms. Yoon, our real teacher, is busy taking care of her brand-new baby. Sometimes I miss Ms. Yoon so much that I wish she'd come back and keep her baby in a Pack 'n Play by her desk, like Daddy used to do with Cleo.

But for now, we are stuck with Mrs. Flavio. There is a look Mrs. Flavio makes when she's happy with a kid, but she never makes that look at me.

I try to sit still during morning meeting, but she blows out a big breath at me.

I try to sit still through language arts, but someone I love is missing, so I don't care too much about improving my vocabulary.

I try to sit still through science, but my guinea pig is probably dead, so I can't really focus on what rocks are made of.

At lunch, it's hard to eat my sandwich knowing that Crescent got eaten up this morning.

And then it's time for recess. On my way out to the field, I bump into Principal Ramsey.

"Quinny Bumble, you're just the kid I'm looking for. Your father called with a message."

Oh no oh no oh no. Where is Hopper when I need a hand to squeeze?

"Relax—your guinea pig is alive and well. Your dad found it in the mailbox."

I jump for joy so high that I almost fall down. Crescent is alive!

I rush back to the cafeteria. "Hopper Hopper Hopper, he's alive—Walter didn't eat him!"

The lunch ladies look over at me, confused. Nobody else is in here.

So I run outside to recess and look around for Hopper on the field.

17

Sometimes he sits on the stairs and reads, sometimes he runs around with the boys—but sometimes Hopper likes to play with me at recess, by the slide and monkey bars.

I run over to the slide and climb up to look for him in the twisty tube part, where we sometimes hang out together. I look by the monkey bars.

And then I spot Hopper, all the way across the playground.

He's sitting on the Friendship Bench.

What? Hopper never sits on that thing. It's supposed to be for finding new friends, but mostly no one sits on it. I don't, either, because I think the best way of finding new friends is to just go up to a person and talk to them, not sit on some lonely bench by a tree.

Even weirder: Hopper is sitting on the Friendship Bench with Kaitlin, and they're looking at some piece of paper together. *Huh?* He never talks to Kaitlin. She's one of Victoria's friends, and Victoria's friends don't talk to the other kids much. They're usually too busy fussing over Victoria, who's in charge of them for sure.

I can't believe Hopper is doing two new things he never does, all in one day.

"Quinny, we're having a Hula-Hoop contest," says Victoria, who is next to me all of a sudden. "You should enter."

Victoria loves starting contests at recess.

"Victoria, guess what, Crescent is alive! And I can't do your contest because I have to go tell Hopper the good news right this very instant."

I look back over to Hopper. He's got a book out now, and he's showing it to Kaitlin. I don't even know what the name of that book is, but I'm kind of shocked, because Kaitlin is not really into books. All she ever talks about are cats and nail polish and her hip-hop dance class.

"The winner of the Hula-Hoop contest gets a free trip with me to the dine-in movie theater," says Victoria.

My head snaps back to her. "What?"

The dine-in movie theater is in Nutley, which is a big town nearby, and I've never even been to that theater because it's so expensive. I heard they have cushy seats that lean really far back and a menu full of treats, and they bring food right to your seat while you watch the movie.

Still, I'm not so great at Hula-Hooping, and I came in last for Victoria's two other contests (jumping rope and staring-without-blinking). I say no thanks and run over to tell Hopper the good news about Crescent. Plus, I want to hear what he and Kaitlin are talking about.

"Hi, Hopper, guess what, Crescent is alive!"

Hopper looks up at me from the bench, all queasy. He's hiding that paper he was looking at behind his back.

"Daddy found him in our mailbox, can you believe it? Also, what's that paper you're hiding behind your back? Also, hi, Kaitlin, what are you talking to Hopper about, since I've never seen you do that before?"

"Hi," Hopper mumbles.

Kaitlin makes a little smile, but it isn't the nice kind of smile. She looks at Hopper, like it's his job to answer my questions.

"Hopper?" I look at him and wait. But he doesn't show me the piece of paper. He doesn't say what they were talking about or ask me to sit down with them. He won't even look at me now.

"Sorry, it's kind of private," says Kaitlin.

Then Hopper scrunches his eyes shut. I can feel how much he wants me to go away.

And I don't even know what to do next.

Hopper and Kaitlin have a secret, and it's more important than me, I guess.

Then a soccer ball hits my leg, and there's my answer for what to do next. I turn away from Hopper and run that ball over toward the goal, and Alex is on my tail, and he shouts out something rude, but that just makes me run faster, and I'm in the mix with Caleb and Xander and everybody out on the field now, and I'm kicking that ball and knocking into boys everywhere. Alex steals the ball back from me, but I speed up after him and force all my hurt from Hopper *down down down* into my ferocious feet, and the harder my heart pumps the calmer my head feels, and I try to swipe that ball back from Alex, and he laughs, but he laughs too soon, because—THWACK! SLAM! SPLAT!—he goes down and that ball is mine and I kick it into the net.

GOAL!

Boy, do I love beating the boys at their own soccer game.

Recess is definitely the best thing in life. Too bad it doesn't last all day.

Four

Hopper

When I open my eyes, I see Quinny running with a bunch of kids out on the field. And I'm still sitting here on the Friendship Bench with Kaitlin, who's not even my friend.

The yard guard's screechy whistle pricks at my ears. Recess is over.

Kaitlin grabs the Smart List back from me, scrunches it tiny in her fist again, and leaves.

Everybody gets in line. I want to talk to Quinny—I want to say sorry for ignoring her before—but she is surrounded by other kids by the time I get to the line.

Maybe I can catch her in the hall before class starts.

I try to, but there are still too many kids around her, talking in a tornado of words.

And then Mrs. Flavio starts class, and everyone has to be quiet again.

In math, we begin a unit on decimals, and Quinny gets this zombie look on her face.

In social studies, we split up into small groups to start a project on Alaskan Inuits, and Mrs. Flavio doesn't put Quinny in my group.

In art, we draw fruit bowls and Mr. Díaz puts Quinny on a private island since she talks more than she draws.

In chorus, I'm in the back row and Quinny is up front, too far away to talk to. Ms. Bing tells me to stand up straight. That's pretty much all she ever says to me. We've been doing a lot of extra chorus practices lately because the Winter Holiday Assembly is coming up and our grade is singing "Jingle Bells" and "Dreidel Dreidel Dreidel" in it.

Today in chorus Ms. Bing is picking people to do the special instrument parts, and she picks Quinny to do wood block for "Jingle Bells." She always gives the special parts to the same bunch of kids she likes best. (I'm not one of them.)

Quinny gets so excited she starts shaking and squealing and hopping up and down.

I look over at her, but when her eyes notice mine, they go cold and look away.

"Wait, Big Mouth got picked to make extra noise? What a surprise," says Alex, and people around him laugh, because people around Alex always laugh when he makes dumb comments. It's one of the perks of being Alex Delgado.

Quinny hollers out the words to "Jingle Bells" as she bangs that wood block up front.

I mumble the words as I slouch in the back. I glance at the tall, quiet girl at the end of my row, who slouches even more than me and picks at her nails. Her name is Juniper and she doesn't even sing—she just mouths the words. Juniper is lucky since Ms. Bing notices her even less than she notices me.

After chorus, Quinny keeps ignoring me for the rest of the afternoon.

I decide to be patient. She and I will ride the bus home together. We have assigned seats right next to each other, so I'll have a chance to make up with her then.

If only I knew what to say.

Five

Quinny

The opposite of recess is called math.

Good-bye soccer ball, hello whiteboard.

Today we're doing a new unit on decimals, which are like fractions but even worse, and Mrs. Flavio has way too much pep in her step as she writes on the board. She's wearing a dress with numbers all over it, which is worse than a dress with mosquitoes all over it, if you ask me.

I glance at Hopper. He's sitting up straight and scrunching his forehead, and his looking-looking eyes pay all their attention to that whiteboard. He looks much happier to see those decimals than he was to see me at recess, that's for sure. I get a sour feeling in my mouth.

Those decimals keep piling up on the whiteboard, and Mrs. Flavio keeps moving the little dots between the numbers, only I keep losing track of those dots. My eyes just want to take a break and look out the window, but Mrs. Flavio has stuck me in the front, so if my head turns she'll say, *Quinny, show me where your eyes should be?* I cross my fingers and my ankles that she doesn't call on me, since I have no clue what she's writing, except that it's numbers and dots.

I hold my breath and wait and wait, and finally math stops and social studies starts. I'm excited to start talking about Alaskan Inuits, because at least you can use words to do that.

Later, in chorus, my day gets better when Ms. Bing picks me to bang the wood block while everyone sings "Jingle Bells"—which we're practicing for the Winter Holiday Assembly that's coming up. Banging things is definitely one of my strengths!

I'm in a great mood after chorus, but Mrs. Flavio does her best to change that. At dismissal she hands out a flyer that's going home in backpacks, and it says:

Greetings WVES Families,

As the winter holidays approach, this is a reminder that no cookies or sweets will be allowed at class parties, due to the new school policy prohibiting food in classrooms. This aligns with our new district policy eliminating dessert from hot lunch and adding extra vegetables and fruit. Thank you for your cooperation as we strive to make WVES a healthier community. Happy Holidays!

Principal Ramsey

I read that flyer again in case my eyeballs were playing tricks on me. Happy Holidays—is he kidding? This is the frowniest news to ever go home in backpacks! And I did *not* give anybody my cooperation for it.

"But Mrs. Flavio," I blurt out. "Cookies are a really important part of school."

"Quinny, settle down."

"You can't just take cookies away from innocent kids. Birthdays will never be the same. And what are we going to do for a winter holiday party? I always bake coconut snowballs—"

"We made candy-cane cookies for last year's holiday party," says Kaitlin.

"My mom always buys sugar cookies," says Xander. "And then she puts them on a plate and sends them in like she baked them at home."

"Oh, sugar cookies are the best," I inform Xander. "No matter where they were born."

"That's enough, everyone," snaps Mrs. Flavio. "This is part of a new district-wide food policy and it's for your own good. Now pipe down, it's time to line up for dismissal."

Mrs. Flavio starts separating us into *busser*, *walker*, and *aftercare* lines. But I have to go find Principal Ramsey and inform him that these new food rules are just plain cruel! How are we supposed to have a winter holiday party without my famous coconut snowball cookies?

I zoom down the hall, away from everyone in the bussers line.

"Quinny? Quinny, wait!" It's Victoria now, behind me. "Where are you going?"

"To find Principal Ramsey and stand up for our cookie rights, of course."

"Did you forget? Skating class starts today. Masha's driving us to the rink."

Victoria pulls me back toward the lockers, where she stops to get her bag.

Did I actually agree to take an ice-skating class with her? I guess so, since I kind of remember saying okay, but I didn't realize it was today. And my parents must have forgotten.

I suddenly feel a poke on my shoulder, from behind.

"Quinny?"

I turn around. It's Hopper. I get that sour feeling in my mouth again. At recess Hopper cared more about talking to Kaitlin than to me. Whatever they were saying looked like a secret, and I don't like secrets that leave me out.

"I . . . uh . . ." he starts. "I just . . ."

If he has something to say, why doesn't he just say it?

"Aren't you riding the . . . ?" he finally murmurs.

"Look, Hopper, I'm super sad about all the cookies being canceled and now I have to go skating

31

with Victoria—so whatever you're trying to say, please just spit it out."

Hopper looks at Victoria. He looks at me. He doesn't spit anything out.

"Hopper, I don't even know what you're trying to say, since you won't actually say it, so why don't you just go tell Kaitlin, since you loved talking to her so much at recess. Bye!"

Hopper steps back. He looks at me, all shaky.

Victoria takes my arm again. "Forget about him, he's being so weird. Masha's waiting—we don't want to be late for our very first skating class."

Masha is the lady who takes care of Victoria while her dad works, and she's waiting over by a big black car. She's very calm, and says she'll call my dad to remind him about skating.

"I can't believe you've never been skating before," says Victoria as we get in her car. "I can already do a one-foot glide. I was going to do private lessons, but then I thought we should do an activity together to work on our friendship, which I think still needs work, don't you?"

I think all my friendships need some work,

to be honest. The way today went with Hopper makes my stomach burn, and I don't even know what happened exactly.

From the front seat, Masha hands us two bento boxes full of dairy-free, nut-free snacks (because Victoria is allergic) and then we drive off to the rink so that Victoria and I can work on our friendship—or maybe just so she can show off her one-foot glide.

I turn and look out the back window at Hopper, in the bussers line now, staring at his shoes. He's the one who was rude at recess, so why am I the one feeling guilty all of a sudden?

Six

Hopper

". . . so why don't you just go tell Kaitlin, since you loved talking to her so much at recess. Bye!"

Bye. The way Quinny says it feels like a kick in the chest.

Then she walks away with Victoria.

I wasn't trying to make Quinny upset at recess. I didn't plan on sitting on the Friendship Bench or talking to Kaitlin. I was just trying to tie my shoe. And I didn't plan on hiding that Smart List behind my back. I just didn't want her to see it and feel hurt.

I watch Quinny walk away with Victoria, who made the Smart List in the first place.

Quinny thinks Victoria is her friend.

But a true friend would never make a list like that.

Quinny gets into Victoria's car and looks over at me with a scowl as the door shuts. She thought I was keeping a secret from her at recess, and she was right.

I wish there was a way to tell her the truth about that secret.

Without hurting her feelings.

Seven

Quinny

Victoria and I get to the Whisper Valley Ice Palace and we sign in at the table and get these big yellow stickers that prove we are in the 4 p.m. learn-to-skate class with Coach Zadie.

I've never had a real live skating coach before! Plus, there is something special about a person whose name starts with a *Z*, so I'm already excited before I even meet her.

Masha takes us to the locker room and Victoria changes into a fancy outfit from her fancy skating bag. I stay in my comfy-loose pants, and stick that nice yellow sticker on my T-shirt (right over the jelly stain from breakfast, because I want to make a good impression on Coach Zadie).

Victoria laces up her shiny white skates with pom-pom laces. I wait in the rental skate line and a lady hands me a pair of floppy brown skates that smell . . . interesting.

"Excuse me, why were you spraying hairspray into the skates?" I ask the lady.

"That's foot odor spray," she says. "So the skates don't stink."

"People who rent skates usually have stinky feet," adds Victoria, who is all of a sudden much taller now. "That's why I got my very own skates."

She kicks a leg up, to show me the perfect white skates I already knew she had.

For a second, I forget why I ever thought skating with Victoria would be fun.

I go sit down and try to lace up my rental skates full of stink spray. It's not as easy as it looks. And Masha is across the room, on her phone. "Here," says Victoria. "I'll do it."

She laces up my skates no problem, and when I stand up I am much taller, too.

I am practically teenager-tall!

"Let's go, we don't want to be late," says Victoria.

I step after her in my clunky stilt-skates, and we get closer to the ice, where the light is brighter and the air is colder and smells a little weird and rubbery. The ceiling is also much taller over the ice, with all these crisscross metal beams up high—like monkey bars for a giant! Victoria steps onto the ice, and then it's my turn. I know how to tap-dance and chicken-dance, and I'm an expert at tae kwon do kicks and soccer kicks. How hard can this skating stuff be?

I take a breath. I take a step.

Splat!

The ice is practically up my nose now. Pain buzzes my bottom and pinches my elbow, and I close my eyes to push my tears back to wherever they came from.

"Quinny, are you okay?" Victoria's voice is calm in my ear.

"Fine, fine! Everything's great!"

I climb back up onto my hands and knees, and then grab on to the boards—oh, these beautiful, amazing boards, which I'm never, ever going to let go of.

"It's okay, everybody falls at first," says Victoria. "Just get up and keep going."

"I know, I am." I inchworm along the boards, grabbing on with both shaky hands.

"Come on, you're holding up traffic," she says.

I look behind me at the line of kids who got on after me and are also clinging to the boards, or are down on their bottoms, looking shocked. That makes me feel a little better.

I finally catch up to Victoria at the meeting spot for our class and there's Coach Zadie, and she is all pizazzy—her leggings have confetti on them and her smile takes up most of her face and her eyebrows look really kind, so I think we'll get along great.

She is also an amazing skater. Coach Zadie shows us how to take marching steps and use our arms to help us balance. She shows us a two-foot glide and a one-foot glide. She shows us how to turn on two feet, and then how to turn on just one foot, which is called a three-turn, even though no one has three feet. She shows us swoopy swizzles and a graceful figure eight.

"These are some of the fun skating elements we'll be learning," says Coach Zadie. "Let's get started. Take a step and start marching . . . march, march, march! Then let yourself glide."

I let go of the boards again and take a little step. And a second step and a third, and then I stop stepping and I'm . . . gliding. I'm really, truly, absolutely gliding along the ice!

My glide is working out so well that I decide to turn it into a swizzle. It looked pretty cool when Coach Zadie did it, plus I like the way *swizzle* sounds.

I can do the first part of a swizzle just fine—where your skates swoop farther apart. But bringing them back together is a teensy bit harder. My skates just keep going farther and farther apart. I'm almost doing the splits on ice now—help!

Luckily, Victoria comes over and pulls me back up from that scary swizzle.

Next comes the most boring part of skating: Coach Zadie explains how to stop. We have to glide, then bend our knees and make a pizza-slice shape with our skates, like a pointy triangle. But

I think it'd be more fun to crash into the boards
and then go eat a real pizza.

I point this out to Coach Zadie and she smiles.
"What's your name again, sweetie?"

"Quinny." I point to my sticker, which is covered up a little bit by all my hair.

"Well, Quinny . . . learning how to stop safely
is one of the fundamentals of skating."

If you ask me, stopping is one of the *no-fun*damentals of skating.

Still, we spend the whole lesson doing things Coach Zadie's way.

We spend more time learning how to *stop* skating than *start* skating. Learning how to fall down "the right way" instead of how NOT to fall.

"Why is she teaching us how to fall down?" I say to Victoria. "I thought the reason for lessons was to learn how NOT to fall."

"Shhh," replies Victoria. "I'm concentrating."

"And why bother learning to stop with all these boards around us? They're perfect for crashing into! Or you could just grab on to someone for a tiny second to slow down."

Even though Coach Zadie is obsessed with safety and *no-fun*damentals, I still like the way she smiles and encourages us. I like the way this rink feels open and big, like there's enough room for me to use all my energy. And I *love* the way the rink even has its own special truck, a Zamboni, which gives the ice a little shower to smooth it after we scratch it up with our skates.

But the best thing about skating is . . . the giant, twisty hot pretzels at the snack bar!

We go to that snack bar after class and I say a giant thank-you to Masha for getting me a giant pretzel. But when I sit with Victoria and take a bite, I realize something's wrong.

This pretzel is hard as a hockey puck. I bang it against the table. "Bummer."

"Hold on." Victoria grabs my pretzel and goes back to the snack-bar man.

"Hello. My friend got a stale pretzel that's too hard to eat. We'd like a fresh one, please."

The snack-bar man stares down at Victoria.

"Thank you in advance for your help," she adds.

Since Victoria already thanked him for his help, the man has no choice but to help.

Wow, I'm going to try this out with Mom. *Thank you in advance for that candy bar. Thank you in advance for that awesome new green bike with an orange-polka-dot basket.*

Victoria comes back to our table with a pillowy-fresh, steamy-hot new pretzel.

"Thank you so much, Victoria!" I rip apart my perfect pretzel and offer her a chunk.

"No thank you, remember I'm on a gluten-free diet," she says.

I don't understand this exactly, but it has to do with her allergies.

Victoria eats pear and goat-cheese circles from her bento box while I chomp on my pretzel. I notice a boy at another table eating a big cookie. And that reminds me I'm still upset.

"Can you believe they're taking cookies away from us in school? It's so unfair."

"Sweets aren't healthy," says Victoria. "We talked about this on student council."

"But remember how last week Nidhi brought in red velvet cupcakes for her birthday?"

"No, because I'm allergic to dairy and didn't eat one."

"Okay, but—"

"Quinny, lots of kids are allergic to dairy or nuts in cookies—and they have rights, too. Also, some people have diabetes, which makes it dangerous for them to eat sugar."

"No one's *forcing* anyone to eat sugar, but cookies shouldn't be against the law—"

"Having junk food around makes it harder for everyone to make healthy choices. Trust me, even if you don't have diabetes, you shouldn't eat sugar. Sugar is poison."

"What?"

"It's true. I read that in one of Masha's food magazines."

But I don't believe Victoria. If sugar was poison, then I'd be dead by now, for sure.

We finish our snack just as the Zamboni finishes giving the rink a shower. The ice is all smooth and shiny now, and so swimming-pool-ish that I could jump right into it. Tons of people burst through the swingy half doors for the next part of skating, which is called Public Session.

It turns out that Public Sessions are very, very, extra-very different from learn-to-skate classes. There are more kids and fewer rules. There's loud music, and this excited feeling, like anything is possible, and you can go as fast as you want—it's like an obstacle course made out of people! As long as you don't bug the rink guards in the orange jackets, of course. They have really loud whistles and they're not afraid to use them.

I zoom around and around that rink, faster and faster. Victoria stays in the middle of the ice, practicing her one-foot glide. Her skates are wobbly, but her face is determined. Her one-foot glide turns into a one-butt fall, but she gets right back up and keeps going.

"Go, Victoria!" I wave as I zoom past.

The faster I go, the less wobbly I am, and I get this *wheeee* feeling as I turn the corners. Maybe next time I'll try hockey skates. The kids wearing those are zooming around the fastest.

The crowd of people skating around the rink is getting bigger and noisier, but I notice that Victoria is still all by herself practicing tricks in the middle of the ice.

And that's when it hits me—the most amazing idea! Principal Ramsey may not listen to just one kid all by herself, but if I start a petition signed by ALL the kids at school, then he'll HAVE to save cookies from being kicked out. (A petition is a letter that you write asking for something unfair to change, and it's signed by a bunch of people who agree. I know this, because Mom wrote one last month, asking for some workers at her college to get paid more money.)

"Victoria?!" I zoom over toward the middle of the rink to share my exciting petition idea.

But just then, someone else comes around the curve fast, a bigger boy, and he's headed straight for . . . me? No, of course not. He'll get out of my way, for sure.

But he's too busy joking with his friends to even notice me. Which means I have to get out of his way. Except my skates forget how to do that, and I don't remember how Coach Zadie taught us to stop. My balance goes backward and my body turns into a floppy noodle and that big boy is getting closer and he's coming straight at me and *aaaaaaaagh no no no—*

Eight

Hopper

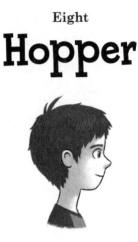

Quinny isn't at the bus stop again on Tuesday. That's two mornings in a row.

When I get to school she's not there, either. By the lockers, I find out why.

Victoria is whispering in a way that isn't really a whisper, but a voice she wants everyone around her to hear. "And then she . . . big crash . . . couldn't even make a pizza stop . . . the guard tried . . . but the . . . crying . . . big bruise on her . . . broken . . . you should've heard her scream. . . ."

I move a little closer. But all I can figure out is that there was some kind of accident at the skating rink yesterday. Where is Quinny now? Victoria doesn't seem to know, either.

I don't know what to think. Is Quinny okay? When is she coming back to school? *Is* she coming back? I try to picture school without Quinny, and I can't do it—my mind goes blank.

After morning meeting, I hear Alex repeat Victoria's story to Caleb, but in his version, a hockey stick hit Quinny in the face and blood gushed out of her nose like a waterfall. Later, on the way to gym, McKayla tells Xander she heard Quinny broke her leg and got taken away in an ambulance with sirens. The way people are talking, Quinny will probably be dead before lunch.

I don't know what the truth is. It doesn't seem like anyone else does, either.

At recess, I don't feel like running or kicking or tagging people.

I'm about to go and sit on the steps with my book, but then I decide to go back to the Friendship Bench instead. It's more comfortable there, and quieter, and shadier, too.

Kaitlin doesn't come by the bench like she did yesterday. She's on the field jumping rope with

Victoria, but she doesn't look too relaxed. She makes recess look more like work.

I spend recess reading. And looking around, since I can see the whole field from here.

Izzy is sitting behind the sycamore tree.

Buck is standing by the door to the school, looking straight up at the sky.

That quiet girl Juniper is walking on the edge of the field, dragging her fingers across the fence. Her eyes are half closed, like she's watching a private movie inside her eyelids.

Some people want to be alone at recess. I'm one of them, a lot of the time.

But I didn't realize there were so many others.

After my best friend, Owen, moved away last year, I started spending recess by myself. I didn't want another friend. I didn't want to admit I wanted one, at least—not until Quinny moved in next door and forced me to be her friend. Maybe that's why no one sits on the Friendship Bench. It's hard to show the world you're lonely. It's hard to say you need a friend.

Even if you need one so badly it hurts to breathe.

After the recess whistle blows, Kaitlin passes by me on her way to line up. Today she's wearing a headband with cat ears, and it makes me want to draw whiskers on her cheeks.

"I know that one." She gestures to my book. "My mom got it for me, it was sooo boring."

The other girls with her laugh. At the book, or maybe at me.

"Hey, I saw the movie they made of that book," says Caleb, in line behind me.

"Me, too," says Juniper, behind him.

Caleb and I both turn to look at her, because Juniper barely ever says a thing.

"The book was better," she murmurs.

Nine

Quinny

My Tuesday morning is full of tragedy, and then Daddy drops me at school just in time to miss recess and sit still for math. Oh, yay.

Mrs. Flavio is up at the whiteboard again putting numbers into bunk beds (that's called fractions) and then mixing them up with a bunch of decimal dot numbers. My brain has to squint to figure out what she is talking about. Plus, Hopper isn't in class today, which makes me even less happy to be here.

"Mrs. Flavio, can I go to the bathroom?" I call out.

Then I remember to raise my hand. You're supposed to do that *before* you ask your question, but maybe she won't notice I did it in the wrong order.

Mrs. Flavio leans down and looks me in the eye. It's terrifying stuff.

"I find it interesting, Quinny, that every time I mention decimals, you feel the sudden urge to use the restroom."

"I'm not sure it's that interesting, Mrs. Flavio. When you gotta go, you gotta go."

She finally says *okay-but-come-right-back-no-dawdling*, and I get a hall pass and go to the bathroom and I sit there in the stall and wait until I'm pretty sure decimals is almost over.

(If Mom knew I did this, she'd be super upset. That's why I'm never going to tell her.)

When I go back out to the hall, there is a giant surprise waiting for me.

"Hopper Hopper Hopper! It's you."

"It's me," he says.

"What are you doing out here in the hall? And why weren't you in class?"

"Mrs. Flavio needed a responsible person to take a note to the main office."

"Oh, Hopper, we have so much to catch up on.

53

I'm sorry I was crabby at you yesterday, I thought you and Kaitlin were keeping a secret from me—"

"I was just trying to tie my shoe, not keep secrets. Honest."

"I know that."

"You do?"

"I figured it out last night. It was the cookie flyer, right? Kaitlin showed it to you. . . ."

Hopper looks confused now.

"You knew it'd ruin my recess—plus my whole life—so you hid it behind your back."

"Quinny, what happened at the rink? Everybody was saying you got hurt—"

"Oh, nothing, I just crashed into a kid who was ten feet tall. But I was fine and went home and everything, but this morning my arm really hurt, so Daddy took me to Urgent Care for an X-ray, but the meanie doctor wouldn't even give me a cast, he said it was just a sprain."

"Well, I'm glad you're okay."

"I'd be even better if they gave me a cast, because then people could write on it. Hey, speaking of writing, Hopper, can you sign my petition to save the cookies?"

"Your what?"

"It's a petition to ask Principal Ramsey to change his mind and let us have classroom sweets for birthdays and holidays still. Remember how Nidhi brought in red velvet cupcakes for her birthday? And for Christmas did you know Daddy and I always bake coconut snowballs—"

"Uh, sure. I'll sign it."

"Great. And by the way, before you sign that petition, could you also help me write it?"

Ten

Hopper

Writing a petition sounds a lot more complicated than signing a petition.

"Quinny, I don't know anything about making a petition."

"That's okay, neither do I!"

"I'm not even on student council—"

"You don't have to be on student council to do a petition. And Victoria has decided to be enemies with my petition, so I need your help big-time—"

"Quinny, Hopper—what are you guys doing out here?"

We get interrupted by Nurse Mira.

"Sorry, Nurse Mira, top-secret official business."

Quinny holds up her hall pass like it's a police badge, and pulls me into a run, giggling.

On the bus ride home we get to work on the petition. Quinny says words out loud and I write them down. But right away, there's a problem.

"Dear Principal Ramsey," Quinny says. "Weren't Nidhi's birthday cupcakes just so yummy? And wait till you try my coconut snowballs at the winter holiday party! I promise to bring you some extras if you could just let us still have sweets and cookies in class, so please change the rules back, or school will turn into such a frowny, miserable place—"

"Quinny—"

"—full of gloomy kids who don't want to come, and then you'll have no customers—"

"Quinny, I think we have to convince him with facts and ideas, not just whining—"

"Fine—Dear Principal Ramsey, it's a fact that cookies are an important part of school, and cookies make kids happy, and happy kids get good grades, so please don't make us all flunk out by stealing all the cookies, because we want our cookies back and we want them back *now!*"

I don't even bother writing any of this down. "Quinny, slow down, that's a lot of words."

"Oh, Hopper, you're right. People look at stuff more than they actually read words, so let's illustrate that petition with lots of yummy cookies!"

"Illustrate it?"

"Yeah, you know, like you could draw cookies and treats on it, because we'll get more people to sign it if it *looks* delicious. And also, we should make signs and walk around the playground. *Save the cookies!* A sign is much bigger than a petition."

I look at Quinny. She's serious. Then she gets this startled look on her face and her eyes zoom toward the bus window. "Hopper!!! Look!" She bounces and points.

Our bus passes Grandpa Gooley's pickup truck, parked by Mrs. Porridge's house. He's got something big in the back, covered by a tarp cloth.

"Hopper, is that . . . are those . . . feathers!?!"

The bus pulls up to our stop and Quinny rushes off and runs over to Grandpa Gooley's truck like her hair is on fire. Her dad doesn't even look shocked as she zooms past him, he just starts walking after her. Catching up to Quinny is something we all have to do.

"Grandpa Gooley!" she cries out. "Is that what I think it is in your truck?"

Brrrp. Bup.

"Take it easy, Quinny. I'm just dropping something off for Mrs. Porridge."

"But Grandpa Gooley, I saw feathers! And I heard clucking!"

"Feathers? What would I be doing with feathers?"

Bipp. Brrrp. Bock.

"Chickens! Hopper, listen, those feathers belong to real live chickens!"

Mrs. Porridge comes over to us. She doesn't look too excited. "These hens weren't supposed to arrive until tomorrow," she snaps.

"My apologies," says Grandpa Gooley.

"I'm not even set up for them yet. And I was hoping to surprise the children."

"Oh, Mrs. Porridge, we're totally surprised," says Quinny. "You said no more chickens ever, and Grandpa Gooley said it's impossible to make you change your mind about anything—"

"Did he, now?"

"But don't worry, we're here to help," says Quinny. "Hopper and I can get that chicken coop cleaned out and ready for these new birds in no time. I'm free right now!"

"Fantastic," says Mrs. Porridge. "Just the nice, calm afternoon I was hoping for."

"Me, too," says Piper. "I'm free right now."

"Mmmptt," says Cleo through her Binky.

"Cleo—spit that thing out. You're a big girl," says Mrs. Porridge.

"We're trying to convince her, believe me," says Quinny's dad.

Brrr bup brrrrripp says something under the tarp in Grandpa Gooley's truck.

"Grandpa Gooley, let us see—come on, come on," cries Quinny. "We need to see those beautiful, brilliant chickens from head to toe right this very minute!"

"Okay, let's do it." Grandpa Gooley grabs the tarp. "Ready to meet your new neighbors?"

Eleven

Quinny

Grandpa Gooley pulls back the tarp, and poof, it's a paradise of feathers! Those chickens flutter and flap their wings, and *bip* and *buup* and *bock* their beaks, and stare out at me from their cages.

"Let them out, Grandpa Gooley, look how excited they are to see me—I need to hug those adorable chickens right this very minute! How many of them are there?"

"Hold your horses, Quinny," says Mrs. Porridge. "We have to be careful they don't run off like what's-her-name . . . that other chicken . . . starts with an *F*?"

Oh, she means Freya, who used to be our fast, ferocious, zebra-striped neighborhood chicken, but over the summer we caught her and brought her back to live with her one true love, Mr. McSoren, in a different town. But then, in a surprise twist, Freya sent us two baby chickens, Disco and Cha-Cha, to adopt—only Disco decided he was a rooster, so he couldn't stay.

"Wait, Grandpa Gooley, did you actually bring Freya back here?"

I get on my tippy-toes, but I don't see any zebra stripes in his pickup truck.

"No, no," says Grandpa Gooley. "Freya and Mr. McSoren are still living over in Milford. These chickens are new. They've got to get used to each other, and to Cha-Cha."

"You mean Cha-Cha *and* Walter. Walter thinks he's a chicken, too," I remind him.

Walter the chicken-cat creeps toward the pickup truck now. Cha-Cha flaps over, too, and leaps onto Walter's back and begins a screechy speech. *BockbockbockbockBOCK.*

"Open the cage!" cries Piper. "Open it!"

Cleo's squealing in her stroller and Daddy leans over to calm her down. "Piper, girls, we don't have time for this," he says. "Quinny, you've got to get ready for soccer."

Oh. I love soccer. But I definitely don't love it more than I love brand-new chickens. Luckily, I figure out just what to say. "My arm—Daddy, I can't go to soccer with a sprain."

Daddy sighs. "You've both got homework, too."

Personally, I think homework stinks very much, and I know Piper does, too. They make us do enough school in school, I don't see why we have to do more school at home.

"Daddy, we need to meet our amazing new chickens first! Please be patient."

"Keep those cages shut for now," says Mrs. Porridge. "Hopper, help me get Cha-Cha and Walter back onto the screened-in porch. Then we'll get extra chicken wire from the shed and set up a separation pen in the coop so we can introduce these new chickens safely and properly."

I don't know what Mrs. Porridge is talking about—a separation pen?

She scoops up Walter, and Hopper picks up Cha-Cha, and they both walk away.

"Grandpa Gooley, these chickens are just fantastic. Let's get them out of the truck, because I think they're a bit smushed in there, plus I can't wait for them to meet Crescent."

"Who?" asks Grandpa Gooley.

"My guinea pig, remember? He's free right now. I'll go get him!"

Grandpa Gooley tugs my sleeve. "You know what, Quinny? These chickens have only been here a couple of minutes. Let's take it slow."

He lifts the first cage out of the truck. It's got a puffy, silly poodle chicken inside, with a shiny-gray feather-duster pouf covering her eyes. But I notice some feathers in her pouf are missing and a few feathers have been plucked off her bottom, too, and her head darts from side to side like she's expecting trouble.

"Wow, that is a very strange-looking poodle chicken."

Piper comes closer to the cage, and Daddy unclicks Cleo from her stroller to come see, too.

"She's called a Silkie," says Grandpa Gooley. "She's not your everyday chicken."

"She's hopping around kind of funny in there," I say. "Is she limping or dancing?"

"A longhorn cow stepped on her. Nearly crushed her, and left her with a slight limp. Her flock on the farm started bullying her after that. That's why some of her feathers are missing."

"Bullying her for getting hurt? Why?? Grandpa Gooley, just let that poor thing out of the cage so we can say hello, please. She looks so worried and trapped. If she was bullied before, she needs to know we're her friends."

"Well . . . I suppose that'd be okay," says Grandpa Gooley. "She seems gentle enough. But first let's see who else we have here. . . ." He unloads a second cage out of the truck.

And inside is the most beautiful hen in the world—her feathers are orange, red, and caramel, she's round and shiny like a pumpkin, plus her face is so happy and awake.

"Let her out, too! She's way too beautiful to be stuck in a cage."

"This one's called a Buff Orpington," says Grandpa Gooley. "They're sweet birds."

Grandpa Gooley lets out both the silly poodle chicken and this beautiful pumpkin chicken, and they scurry out of their cages and peck the ground and look around the world.

Buuup. Bip. Ooop. Erp. Bock.

Cleo laughs and Piper gets down on the ground with them, practically eye to eye.

But there's one last cage on the truck and it's so full of white feathers that I can't tell how many chickens are squeezed in there, all wiggly and crowded. So while everyone is focused on the first two chickens, I reach up and open that third cage—just to give those poor, smushed chickens some air.

But Grandpa Gooley isn't even proud of me for this.

"Quinny, no!" he says.

But it's too late. All those feathers burst out of the cage and a head pops out—just one head, because that big blob of feathers is actually just ONE HUGE CHICKEN.

She's white and fluffy and practically the size of a baby polar bear! Her eyeballs are as big as gumballs and she stomps around in a confused way. It looks like she's got tall, feathery boots on her giant feet, and I can almost feel the earth shake with each stumble-stomp she takes.

"Don't be afraid, she's just a chicken," says Grandpa Gooley. "She's a Brahma, and they do get kind of big."

I'm not afraid—I want to hug that huge, fluffy polar-bear chicken. But Cleo does not. She spits out her Binky and screams. Even though that chicken looks more terrified than terrifying.

Then the gray poodle chicken limps over and grabs Cleo's Binky from the ground.

"No, drop it!" I chase after her, but she limp-runs off with the Binky in her mouth and spreads her wings and flutters up into Mrs. Porridge's fig tree.

That poodle chicken can definitely fly better than she can run.

"Mine, mine, mine!" wails Cleo, reaching up toward the tree. "Binky, mine!"

Piper climbs up into the tree and goes after that poodle chicken.

"Piper, get down," says Daddy, over Cleo's wailing. "Guys, we really have to leave."

But I have a brilliant idea, instead. I go to the screened-in porch and open the door for Walter and Cha-Cha to come back outside.

"Quinny, stop!" calls out Grandpa Gooley. "Mrs. Porridge said Cha-Cha and Walter should stay inside for now."

"But Walter is excellent at climbing trees, and he'll help Piper catch that poodle chicken who stole Cleo's Binky. Walter, go!"

But Walter doesn't run to the tree, like I told him to. He goes over to the other chickens, who are now having a teeny-tiny argument. That pumpkin chicken is pecking at the polar-bear chicken's feathery boots. Walter zooms over to the pumpkin chicken and knocks her flat. Then he hisses at the polar-bear chicken, and she lowers her giant scaredy-bird head.

"No Walter, forget about these chickens on the ground and go get the Binky back from that poodle chicken in the tree!"

The poodle chicken keeps flapping-flying higher up with the Binky, and Piper climbs after her and Cha-Cha is clucking at them from the ground, but she can't fly into the tree.

"Piper, get down from that tree THIS MINUTE!" calls Daddy. He's trying to wrestle crybaby Cleo back into her stroller, but she arches her back so he can't buckle her in.

"Binky Binky, mine mine!"

The Binky thief keeps climbing and Piper keeps following her. I've never seen my sister climb so high up that fig tree, up to where the branches get really skinny.

"Piper, stop, please!" Daddy yells, over Cleo's wailing. His voice sounds scared now.

I look around for Hopper. Piper listens to him better than anyone, but he went off with Mrs. Porridge to do something, I forget what exactly. I wish Hopper would hurry back, because I bet he could get Piper down from the tree.

"Piper, Daddy will build you a tree house if you climb down from there," I call out.

Daddy's head twists over to me. "I will?"

"A tree house with bunk beds. And, he'll let you go to school in your underpants."

"Quinny, please," says Daddy.

Cha-Cha loses interest in the poodle chicken up in the tree and runs over to the pumpkin chicken, with her wings flapping and chest feathers all puffed. In one swoop, she slams that pumpkin chicken on her back.

Swat!

"Cha-Cha, no, you're a dancer, not a fighter," I tell her.

All the chickens are freaking out and Cleo is wailing and Piper is climbing and Grandpa Gooley is running around in a confused squiggle trying to calm everything down.

Then, without asking permission, that giant polar-bear chicken jumps into my arms!

She knocks me down and clings to me so hard I can barely see past all her scared fluffy feathers.

"It's okay, sweetie." I hug that enormous chicken back, even though her nails scratch me and her sneezy feathers tickle my nose. "I'll keep you safe. But could you please move a little? You're sort of crushing my left foot."

I can't feel my foot and I can't see past her feathers, but I can still hear—and what I hear next is the crackle-crunch of a tree branch breaking.

Twelve

Hopper

There's no chicken wire in the shed, so we go down to Mrs. Porridge's basement.

"Aha, there it is!" She finds a tall roll of prickly gray wire near her washing machine. "Why that grandfather of yours hid it down here is a mystery to me."

"Mrs. Porridge, why do we need more chicken wire?" The Chalet des Poulets, which Grandpa Gooley built, is already big enough for all the new chickens just the way it is.

"Why indeed? I certainly have more important things to deal with than chickens. I was in the middle of my winter cleaning when that truckful of feathers so rudely interrupted me."

"Mrs. Porridge, it's not winter yet. Winter doesn't start until December twenty-first."

"Oh pish, close enough."

"Is winter cleaning like spring cleaning? My parents do that every year, and I help."

"Hopper, I never understood why people say *spring cleaning*. In the spring all I want is to be outside in the garden. Colder weather is the proper time to purge and clean. . . ."

Mrs. Porridge's basement looks like it could use a good cleaning. There are boxes and piles of stuff everywhere. Some of those boxes are full of books, I notice—including the old-fashioned kind, with hard, faded library covers. The kind that smell old and good and something else, a smell that makes me feel both safe and curious.

I look through one of the boxes and see a book called *When It Rained Cats and Dogs*. Under it are more ridiculous books: *Letters from a Cat, Why Cats Paint, The School for Cats, Punky Dunk and the Mouse, Cat vs. Human*, and *Dancing with Cats*—that last one has a lady on the cover with her hair sticking straight up, dancing with a cat jumping high in the air.

"I may have had a *slight* obsession with silly cat books, a long time ago," says Mrs. Porridge. "Been meaning to donate those. My shelves upstairs are all full."

These cat books make me think of Kaitlin from school.

They also make me think of a new idea.

I'm about to ask Mrs. Porridge a big question, but wailing from outside interrupts our conversation, and then some shrieking.

"Oh dear," says Mrs. Porridge. "I don't like the sound of that."

She walks up the basement steps and I follow her. We look out the kitchen window.

Cleo is out there sobbing, pounding the ground with her fists. An orange chicken is fighting with Walter and Cha-Cha. Grandpa Gooley tries to break up the fight, but the orange chicken pecks his ankles. Quinny is out there, too, smothered beneath a huge pile of white feathers. Did a pillow explode? No, she's talking to the feathers. Piper is high up in Mrs. Porridge's fig tree, clinging to a swaying branch. Piper's dad is waving and yelling for her to jump into his arms. A gray chicken in a weird puffy wig is even higher up in the tree, chewing something.

"Five minutes, I'm gone just five minutes," snaps Mrs. Porridge. She turns to me, sharply, like I did something bad, too. "You wonder why we need extra chicken wire? To build a separation pen. You've got to keep new chickens separated from each other at first."

"Why?"

"Hopper, don't you get it by now? Chickens are monsters."

"I thought they were dinosaurs."

Mrs. Porridge moves fast now. She grabs a spray bottle from a kitchen cabinet, fills it with water, and hands it to me.

"The orange one," she says. "Aim for between its eyes. Keep spraying and don't stop until you've forced that creature back into its cage. Got it?"

I nod. I've sprayed my big brothers with a water hose before. I can handle this.

Next Mrs. Porridge sloshes a mop in some water. She hurries outside, waving that drippy mop like a weapon. I grab my spray bottle and follow her into battle.

I aim for the orange chicken's face, but just before I press the lever, I hear a—

CRACK!

I look up. It's the tree branch with Piper on it.

Thirteen

Quinny

CRACK! RUSTLE-RUSTLE. CRACK!

I push a bunch of white feathers out of my face and see Piper falling from the fig tree.

Luckily, she lands on Daddy. She knocks him over just a bit, and they roll around in a pile and they almost roll onto that pumpkin chicken, who is fighting Cha-Cha and Walter, and guess what, Hopper is back, and he's spraying the pumpkin chicken from a little spray bottle, but she dodges him and hops away and the water lands on Walter, who does a screechy-meow.

"Hopper Hopper Hopper, you're back! Can you help me get out from under this giant polar-bear chicken, please? But don't scare her, because she's already really scared."

Hopper comes over and sprays my giant chicken in the tushy.

Errrrp!

She jumps off of me, finally, but then the pumpkin chicken comes over and pecks at her feathery boots. Too bad that pumpkin chicken is only beautiful on the outside. Hopper sprays her with his water bottle again, and she backs off my polar-bear chicken. I definitely need to get one of those spray bottles to use on my little sisters.

Mrs. Porridge is over by the fig tree shaking a wet mop up at the gray poodle chicken, and I laugh, because we're all getting wet now, and it's almost as awesome as the time over the summer when we blasted Hopper's brothers with the water hose, except it's November outside now, which means cold water feels a tiny bit colder than it did in July.

The pumpkin chicken bops over to the tree and pecks Mrs. Porridge, but she jabs at it with the handle of her mop. "You've got some nerve, missy," she snaps.

That chicken scrambles away, shaking out her

pretty feathers, all innocent, like *Who me? I didn't peck anybody's ankles.*

"Don't bother looking sweet, that doesn't work on me," adds Mrs. Porridge.

Grandpa Gooley helps Daddy and Piper back up. The poodle chicken comes down from the tree, finally, like nothing crazy just happened. She drops the Binky, and Cleo grabs it.

"No, Cleo!" I call out.

But she sticks that dirty Binky back in her own mouth, without wiping it or anything.

I guess my sister likes the taste of chicken.

Daddy closes his eyes and shakes his head.

"Daddy, relax," I tell him. "The good news is, that's not even the grossest thing Cleo has ever put in her mouth."

Mrs. Porridge shakes her wet mop at Grandpa Gooley now. "What were you thinking, letting these birds out of their cages before we were properly set up? And where on earth did you find them? I ask for a few quiet hens, you bring a bunch of violent, enormous freaks of nature."

"The big one's a Brahma, but I call her a polar-bear chicken," I inform Mrs. Porridge.

"Her family didn't like how large she grew, and didn't want her anymore," says Grandpa Gooley. "Isn't that sad? Such a beautiful creature . . ."

"Hmmmpt. And that ridiculous puffy gray one—a thief who can barely walk. Is it sick?"

"No, she just got stepped on by a cow," I explain. "And then her friends were mean to her because she hops around with a limp now, so Grandpa Gooley brought her to live here."

"Well, send her back. I don't have time to take special care of an injured chicken."

"But Mrs. Porridge, look at her face. Look at how hard she's trying to hop around and still be a chicken. And she flew up into that tree, so we know she has amazing wings! What if she also lays the most amazing eggs and we'll never know because we didn't give her a chance?"

"That giant white one—you can send it back, too. Send them all back."

"Mrs. Porridge, every living creature deserves a chance. If I walked with a limp, would you send me away? Or if I grew into a giant?"

"Bite your tongue, Eleanor Quinston Bumble. Of course not, don't talk such nonsense."

"Quinny has a point," says Grandpa Gooley. "Myrna, in your heart, I know you're a sucker for helping an underdog—"

"You bite your tongue, too," snaps Myrna (aka Mrs. Porridge).

"Or should I say under-chicken?" Grandpa Gooley smiles hopefully.

Mrs. Porridge frowns.

"Okay, this is all my fault for showing up a day early," he says. "Although I did send you a text that the chickens were ready today."

"A text? You sent me a text?" Mrs. Porridge scoffs. "Do I look like the kind of person who constantly checks my *texts*? A phone call would've been the polite, sensible way to—"

"My deepest apologies." Grandpa Gooley hangs his head. "But don't take it out on these poor confused chickens—they need a home. Let's get the separation pens up in the coop and—"

"What exactly *is* a separation pen?" I ask.

"It's the safest way to get a group of new chickens used to each other," says Grandpa Gooley. "They'll be able to see, but not bother each other, through the chicken wire. You leave it up for a few days . . . it helps the chickens relax, and start to establish a pecking order."

"But we don't *want* them to peck at each other," I point out.

Grandpa Gooley chuckles. "No, Quinny, *pecking order* refers to how a flock decides on a chicken in charge, and where everyone fits into the group."

"I think the chicken in charge will probably be the mean orange one," says Hopper.

"Or the polar-bear chicken, because it's huge," I say. "Or maybe even Walter, since he's the only one who's a cat."

"It's not always size that matters—it's personality," says Mrs. Porridge.

"Girls, we really need to go," says Daddy. "Remember, homework? Piper, you have worksheets to finish from yesterday, still."

"Daddy, why does Piper even have homework? I never had any in kindergarten."

"You went to a different school for kindergarten, Quinny. Whisper Valley Elementary has its own rules, and they want kids to start reading and writing sooner."

"Why?" I ask.

Daddy shrugs. "That's an excellent question. We can discuss it on the way home."

"But we've got three new chickens to name! And Crescent hasn't even met them yet—"

"Quinny—"

"Plus, they look hungry, so I really think we need to feed them a snack. Luckily, I didn't eat any of the healthy stuff in my lunch box today, so they can have it all right now!"

"Quinny, I'm taking off, too, just as soon as I get these separation pens up," says Grandpa Gooley. "The chickens could use a little quiet time. Promise me you'll all help Mrs. Porridge keep things running smoothly around here, and I bet they'll settle down very soon."

"Of course we will!" I inform him. "Look how calm those chickens are now. I think they used up all their bad behavior."

"Doubt it," says Mrs. Porridge. "It usually takes a flock of chickens a few days to settle in and establish a pecking order. And that's with *normal* chickens. With this bottom-of-the-barrel bunch of hopeless misfits, who knows how bad it'll get?"

Well, I don't care if these are bottom-of-the-barrel, not-normal, misfit chickens. I just know they're going to live cluckily-ever-after in the Chalet des Poulets, with Cha-Cha and Walter, and make a spectacular four-chicken/one-cat family.

Normal = boring, if you ask me.

"Mrs. Porridge, I promise you, these interesting and gorgeous chickens will figure it out. And don't forget the best part."

"Which part is that, Quinny? The part where I'm stuck with a chicken the size of a bear lurking through my garden? Or a vicious little beauty who pecks me to a bloody pulp?"

"No, Mrs. Porridge, the best part is these are all grown-up chickens already! And you know what big grown-up chickens make?"

"Grown-up chicken poop."

"Eggs!! We'll *finally* have some fresh eggs around here!"

Fourteen

Hopper

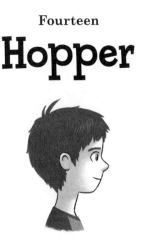

After Quinny leaves, and the chickens are safe in their separation pens, I explain my big idea to Mrs. Porridge.

"Interesting," she says. "Help yourself, Hopper—you'll be doing me a favor."

Then I go home and explain my big idea to Mom.

"That old wagon? I don't see why not—it's just sitting there in the garage," she says. "I think it's a great idea, Hopper, but you should get permission from Principal Ramsey first."

I know that.

I ask permission to go onto Mom's computer so I can ask permission from the principal.

Because sometimes it's easier for me to type a question than to say it out loud.

Mom says okay, and logs me onto her e-mail. (This fall she changed her password from PASSWORD to REPPOH. It took me four seconds to figure it out, but she doesn't know I did.)

The great thing about typing is that it lets you go back and check what you're saying, and even change it. When you talk, you only get one chance, and if you don't say it right or if people aren't listening, then it's all a waste.

I thank Mom for letting me use her computer and I start typing:

To: sramsey@wves.edu
From: carolinegrey@zmail.com
Tuesday, Nov 13; 4:12 p.m.

Principal Ramsey,
  This is Hopper Grey. I am typing on my mom's computer.
  I have a question. Can I paint the Friendship Bench a different color, and call it the Books & Buddies Bench? I think this will help more kids use it. It would give them

an excuse to sit there, without saying they don't have any friends. People who like to read can sit there and read, or talk about books, because sometimes playing tag or soccer can get too crazy. It could be another place to go if you don't want to play with a lot of people, but don't want to be alone either. Or if you want to be alone, but kind of with other people who want to be alone, too.

I also think having a Books & Buddies Bench on the playground is a good example of "reading without walls," which was on a poster I once saw in the library. I liked that poster a lot. Mr. Brolin used to have it up, but it got ripped and I don't know where it is now.

If you say yes, my neighbor Mrs. Porridge will let me have her leftover paint and brushes and a lot of books from her basement. Mom said I could have our old wagon, too, since it's just sitting in our garage. We could fill the wagon with books and roll it back and forth from school to the bench at recess.

This is just an idea, but I hope you say yes.

And my last sentence is: thank you for reading my e-mail.

Your student,
Hopper Grey

Fifteen

Quinny

Instead of doing my boring homework, I decide to work on my exciting petition. I write and write . . . and write some more. I have a lot to say about cookies.

When I'm done, the petition is four pages (front and back!), and I sign my name at the end, and staple some extra pages to it, so people who agree with me can write their autographs.

Principal Ramsey is going to be so impressed. I bring the petition downstairs to show Mom.

"Wow, Quinny, this is very . . . long," she says. "How's your homework going?"

Ugh. How can Mom talk about dreary home-work when I'm trying to do something really important here, by sticking up for cookies in school?

"Mom, did I tell you the best part? Hopper is going to decorate the petition with cookie art, to make it extra yummy. When Principal Ramsey reads it, he'll change the rules for sure."

Mom looks a little skeptical, but I get my whole family to sign the petition. Piper's printing is wobbly and Cleo's fingerprint is sticky (I dipped her finger in a little paint, since she can't write yet), and my parents' autographs look just like messy scribbles. I also want to get Crescent to sign it with her tiny little furry paw print, but Mom says *enough is enough* and sends me back upstairs to finish my homework. Which I guess means I have to start it in the first place.

On the bus Wednesday morning, I can't wait to show Hopper my petition.

"Hopper Hopper Hopper, guess what? I have some exciting news."

"Me, too," he says.

Before I can even show him my petition, he tells me his idea for changing the Friendship

Bench into a Books & Buddies Bench, and how Principal Ramsey e-mailed back this morning to say yes. He tells me how Kaitlin gave him the idea for it at recess, which I think is funny.

"Oh, Hopper, you are never going to get Kaitlin to sit and read a book at recess. All she cares about is nail polish and hip-hop dancing and her cat named Selena."

"Look what I found in Mrs. Porridge's basement," he says.

He shows me a funny book about cats. I have to admit Kaitlin might like it.

"Mrs. Porridge said I could take it," he says. "There were tons of other books down there, and she said I could borrow them all, for good, and we could go to garage sales for more and—"

"Hopper, breathe!" I laugh. It's excellent advice—I get it from people all the time.

"Can you help me paint the bench at recess?" he asks. "Mrs. Porridge will bring some old paint cans from her basement. Mom's going to drop off our old wagon to hold the books."

"Sure, but you have to draw some cookies on my petition first. I finished writing it last night and

I need some really professional cookies, because I want people to go WOW."

I show him the petition. He says the same thing Mom said—it's kind of long. He starts to give me some advice about making it shorter, but the petition is already finished, so it's too late.

"Hopper, thanks for your help, but I already wrote it all down in pen and can't erase it, so can we just focus on making the petition look delicious?"

He shrugs and draws a few cookies on it. And they definitely look good enough to eat.

Then I ask everyone on the bus for their autograph. I even ask Jeanie, our driver, when I get off. Plus Paul, the crossing guard by our school. He laughs, but says okay. That's fourteen autographs before I even get inside the building.

When Principal Ramsey sees this petition, he won't know what hit him!

Sixteen

Hopper

At recess on Thursday, Caleb helps me paint. We turn the Friendship Bench into the Books & Buddies Bench.

Alex would rather play tag than paint. He makes fun of us. But Caleb ignores him, and that makes it easier for me to ignore him, too.

Xander comes over to watch us paint. He looks like he can't decide whether to make fun of me, like Alex, or help me paint, like Caleb. I pull out another paintbrush and offer it to him. Mrs. Porridge gave me lots of brushes, along with these cans of green paint from her basement.

The person I really wish would help me paint is Quinny. But she's been running around at recess for the past couple of days getting signatures on her cookie petition. I signed it, too. Even though she didn't use any of my advice. Her petition is still very long and sloppy. I don't think Principal Ramsey will like it. But Quinny is getting a lot of kids to sign it.

Not Victoria, though. I watch Victoria and Quinny talking by the monkey bars.

It does not look like a happy conversation. Then they walk in separate directions. Some of the girls follow Quinny. Some follow Victoria. Some stand there, looking confused.

I try to focus on painting this bench. And on Xander and Caleb, who are helping me.

We're making the new words *Books* and *Buddies* big and easy to see.

Quinny comes by a few moments later.

"Wow, that new bench looks great, Hopper. Did you know green is my favorite color? But you should add some orange, too, because that's my other favorite color. Plus, add some polka dots, because they make people happy."

I'm not a big fan of polka dots. But I add a few inside the two *O*s in *Books*, just for her.

"Want to help?" I offer Quinny my last spare brush.

"Thanks, Hopper. But I still have to get more people to autograph my cookie petition. Look how many I got so far, even though Victoria is enemies with my petition for some reason."

Some of the signatures are hard to read. Some are just first names. Some I don't even recognize from school. I have more advice for her, but I don't give it. She won't listen anyway.

"By the way, I love your wagon," she says. "A red wagon full of books is the best. That's so great your mom brought it to school for you."

Mom used to pull me and my brothers around in this wagon when we were little. Now I'll use it to bring books from inside school out to the Books & Buddies Bench at recess every day.

"But you know what? You should keep these books out here all the time," says Quinny. "That way people would get used to them. And if you're absent they'd still be out here."

"The books will get ruined if I leave them outside all the time."

"Oh, oh, I know!" Quinny hops. "We could build

a chicken coop for those books! Bock bock *books*!
Bock bock *books*!" She cracks herself up so much
she loses her balance.

Caleb and Xander smirk at each other. I know
what they're thinking.

But a chicken coop for books makes sense, in a
Quinny kind of way.

A little wooden house to keep the books safe
and dry on the playground.

And then I remember my friend Owen. His
cousin had something like that in front of his
house. It was called . . . it was called something. . . .
I try to remember the name.

It was called a Little Free Library.

A long time ago, back in first grade, we went
to visit Owen's cousin and the Little Free Library
was sitting there on their grass. It was bigger
than a birdhouse, smaller than a stove, and filled
with books. Books you could borrow and return
anytime, without paying a fine. Books you could
even keep. That was the wildest part. There was
no way to get in trouble with those books.

"A chicken coop for books is called a Little Free
Library. Owen's cousin had one."

"Who?" Quinny asks.

I remind her about Owen, who moved away before she moved to town. He liked to read as much as I do. He liked science and making things, like I do. It hurts to think about how Owen left, but now that I have Quinny, it hurts less than it used to.

I tell her about the Little Free Library that I saw at Owen's cousin's house.

And the more I talk, the more Quinny bops around, all excited.

"You're right, Hopper, that sounds just like a chicken coop for books. We definitely need to get a Little Free Library for the playground."

"I'll make one," I say. "I'll see if Grandpa Gooley has any extra wood from when he built the Chalet des Poulets."

"You will? Hopper, you're a genius!"

I know how to hammer a nail, but I don't know how to make an entire Little Free Library. But since I just told Quinny I would, I guess I'll have to find a way.

After school Quinny and I go to Mrs. Porridge's house, and see her out getting her mail.

"Mrs. Porridge! How are the chickens doing? Plus, would you sign my cookie petition?"

Quinny whips out her petition. Mrs. Porridge takes a moment to look it over.

"You have got to be kidding me," she finally says.

"I know, isn't it awful how Principal Ramsey hates cookies?"

"Quinny, this petition is sloppy and repetitive. And frankly, the last thing you need in school is a sweet. I can imagine those poor teachers having to deal with all you sugared-up kids."

"Bite your tongue, Mrs. Porridge! Cookies make school a better place."

"We'll just have to agree to disagree on that. Hopper, how did the painting go today?"

"Good. Caleb and Xander helped, and we got about half the bench painted. But I was wondering if you have any extra wood? From when Grandpa Gooley built the chicken coop?"

"Hmm, nope. What are you up to now?"

I explain our new idea to build a Little Free Library near the Books & Buddies Bench. Mrs. Porridge says it sounds like a "fine" idea, but that we're on our own tracking down more wood. "Now, are you kids here to help with the chickens, or to just stand around yakking?"

Poodle, Pumpkin, and Polar Bear (that's what Quinny named the chickens, and I didn't argue) are still stuck in their separation pens in the Chalet des Poulets. Mrs. Porridge doesn't want to put them all together yet, not until they settle down.

But she lets them out now for a little bit, since Quinny and I are here to supervise. And she gives us jobs. Mine is to spray Pumpkin with the water bottle and yell *NO* every time she pecks. Eventually she'll figure out we're in charge of her, not the other way around. Poodle limps around, free-ranging with Cha-Cha and Walter. Polar Bear is still scared and hides in the henhouse. Quinny's job is to try and coax her out.

"Come on out, you big beautiful scaredy-bird," Quinny calls out. "Life is worth living."

Quinny's dad shows up. "Quinny, time for soccer."

"Right now?" She groans. "I'm helping with the chickens. Plus I have a sprained arm, remember?"

"Your sprained arm was strong enough to be doing handstands this morning, remember? Now you signed up to drill with Trevor and Ty's league twice a week—Tuesday and Thursday. If you don't want to go, we should cancel and try to get our money back."

I know Quinny loves playing soccer, she just hates leaving for soccer sometimes.

"No, no, I'll go," she says. "But Daddy, wait, do you have any extra wood we could have? See, Hopper is going to build a chicken coop for all the books at recess and—"

"Quinny, please. Come change and grab your cleats, we're running late."

After Quinny leaves, it's quieter. That makes it easier for me to think.

Maybe we have something in our garage I could use to make a Little Free Library.

I walk over and look. Bikes. Toys. A wrinkled old tent. Tools, grubby garden stuff.

I go inside my house and call Grandpa Gooley. He doesn't have any extra wood, but says he'll try to track some down. "It's a worthy idea, Hopper, but lumber's not cheap."

Then I look on Mom's computer for more ideas.

It turns out there are all kinds of Little Free Libraries out there. People buy them or make them out of anything, even old mailboxes or microwaves. You can also buy a kit that comes with everything you need to make one (but it costs $125), or buy one already put together ($295). Yikes. I cross my fingers that Grandpa Gooley can help us find some free wood.

I get out my sketchbook. I draw a very rough sketch.

Mom comes over to the computer, wearing her exercise clothes and headphones. "Honey, Mrs. Porridge said she'd come over and keep an eye on you. I'm going for a run."

I know Mom's been training for this big running race called the Turkey Trot.

She turns to leave, but I stop her. "Wait, Mom, can I go with you?"

"*You* want to go for a run?" Mom looks amused.

She's never seen me play tag at recess. She doesn't realize I run pretty fast when I try.

"Can we run past the hardware store?" I ask. "I need to stop in and see if they have some stuff

I need for a school project. I want to make a Little Free Library on the school playground."

I show Mom my sketch. She looks impressed and says we can stop and check.

I go get my sneakers on and we leave for a run. I fold up my sketch and take it with me.

We start slow. Then we speed up—but just a little. Mom says she has to pace herself, or she

won't last until the end of the race, which is five kilometers long.

Running is hard work. It also feels good.

We get to the hardware store. Mom waits outside, running in place, while I go in.

I take a deep breath (hard to do when you're already out of breath) and go up to the man at the counter and pretend to have Quinny's personality. "Hello, I need enough wood to build a Little Free Library. It's the size of a big mailbox. Like this sketch. Can you tell me the price?"

The man looks at my sketch. He says the hardware store doesn't sell wood, but a lumberyard does, and it would probably cost about ninety-five dollars for enough wood.

That's a lot of money. And I don't know where there is a lumberyard.

I go back outside and keep running with Mom. We don't go straight home but that's fine. Mom's been taking her Turkey Trot training pretty seriously. This is her first race ever, and she'll run it on Thanksgiving morning. Mom's phone beeps while we run.

"Yay," says Mom, looking at her phone. "Another pledge."

She shows me her phone. Someone just gave her twenty dollars for running the Turkey Trot.

"Cool," I say.

Mom asked her friends to sponsor her for the race, which means donating money to this charity she picked, which feeds hungry people. If she runs the race, they donate money.

We finish our run and walk back home. I'm really tired, but the weird thing is I also have more energy than when I started. Dad is out in the yard with Trevor and Ty. They're back from soccer and horsing around. Trevor is walking our slack line. It's wider than a tightrope, but just as wobbly. Quinny's there, too, doing a handstand. I guess her arm really is all better.

"Thanks for the run," Mom says to me. "We should do this again sometime."

We really should.

Ty grabs Quinny's ankles and swings her out of her handstand. I want to go rescue her, but she doesn't cry—she laughs as he swings her around. I feel happier with my brothers lately. Maybe not happier, but okay-er, which isn't a word, just the truth. I think it's because of Quinny. She's not afraid of them. She shows me how not to be, either.

I go over and step on the slack line. Staying balanced on it is hard. Trevor helps me get steady. When I'm ready to take a step, he knocks me off and laughs. But I don't care—I get back on and try again. I take a couple steps, but then I stop, and stand there, wobbling on it. I feel extra awake all of a sudden, because I just thought of another idea. A gigantic one.

I go up to Dad. "I'm running the Turkey Trot race with Mom."

"What?" He looks down at me, confused.

"I'm going to train with Mom and run the race and raise money to build a Little Free Library on the school playground."

"You are?" Mom looks really surprised. I know the race is only a week away.

"I am," I tell them. It feels good to say that out loud.

The next thing I say feels even better: "Will you guys sponsor me?"

Seventeen

Quinny

The best way to forget about all the math homework I didn't understand this week is . . . Saturday-morning Open Swim with Hopper, of course!

I put my bathing suit on under my clothes and Mom packs my swim cap and towel. Daddy isn't coming, because he's taking Piper and Cleo to a birthday party. (The party is at a zoo and I think he should just leave Piper there for good.) So on the ride to the Y, it's just me, Mom, Hopper, and Hopper's dad, who drives. When I look at our reflection in a store window, it's like we're one family, like Hopper is my very own brother. How awesome would that be!

From the front seat, Hopper's dad says, "So, Quinny, I heard you're making great progress on the field. Coach can't believe you've never played before."

All Hopper's dad talks to me about is soccer. "It's because I used to do a lot of kicking in tae kwon do," I tell him. "Plus, I eat lots of cookies."

"No kidding." He makes a curious face in the car mirror.

"I'm serious, Mr. Grey. Cookies make you happy, and a happy person has stronger kicking muscles than a sour grumpy person, and that's why I started a petition to—"

"Enough about the petition," Mom interrupts me.

But I explain it all to Hopper's dad anyway— and then I whip the petition out of my bag (because I take it everywhere, of course) and I ask for his autograph.

"Quinny, are you sure it counts if the person isn't a student?" says Hopper.

"A person's a person, everyone counts. Mr. Grey, please sign it, cookies are an important part of a balanced diet. And your own son illustrated this petition to make it look extra yummy."

"I'd be happy to sign it, once I stop driving. Good luck, guys—you can do anything you set your minds to." Mr. Grey looks at Hopper when he says this, then at me. "You know, Quinny, Coach thinks you could make the club team next year, with a bit of hard work."

It's interesting what Mr. Grey is saying, but I don't say anything back. The twins do club soccer and it takes up a lot of time (like five afternoons a week!) and it's kind of a big deal. Alex, Caleb, and Maeve at school do it, too. But there's also a less fancy kind of soccer that Caleb told me about, called rec soccer, and it's just once a week. If I want to do other things like skating or swimming, too, then rec soccer might be better for me. But I don't tell Hopper's dad this, no way.

"As for us, we've been focusing more on swimming lately," he says. "I've been having a blast taking Hopper to Open Swim every week. Did he mention he's thinking of joining the Y team?"

"Really?" I look at Hopper to see if it's true, but he's looking out the window, so I can't see the answer. His quiet gives me a clue to the answer, though.

In the Y's locker room, Mom stretches the pinchy-tight, sticky-white swim cap on me. It's a rule that you have to wear a cap in the pool if you have big hair, but—ouch!—my head needs two or three of these caps, I think.

When my hair is finally all trapped in that painful swim cap, I run out to the pool.

"Hopper Hopper Hopper!" I rush over to him standing by the edge of the pool. He's got blue alien-bug eyes and swim trunks with sharks on them.

"Quinny, be careful," says Mom. "No running at the pool."

The lifeguard also beeps his whistle at me. I wave up at him.

Then I crash into Hopper and laugh. "Hi."

"Hi." He smiles a little smile.

And then, oh-so-casually, he pushes me into that pool—and the water is freezing!

I splash and kick. "Get in, Hopper, get in right this minute!"

I swim over to the side of the pool so I can pull at his leg, but he moves away and laughs. I learned to swim when I was little, but there weren't a lot of pools in our neighborhood back in New York. When we moved to Whisper Valley, I was going to take swimming lessons again, but the class was full by the time Mom called, so I kind of taught myself to swim all over again, just enough so that I don't sink to the bottom.

But I am amazed by how great Hopper can swim. He jumps in, headfirst, and it's like he just slips and sneaks right into the water, without even a splash. And then he's under for so long and he pops back up at the opposite end of the pool, like a magic trick!

He spits out a bit of water, like a funny fish, smiles at me, and then goes back under. If Hopper were a Wac-A-Mole, I'd never be able to whack him because he goes faster under the water than my eyes can find him. Then he gets out and jumps back in with his headfirst jump. I love watching him! Hopper has such a slow and calm personality, but such a fast, fishy body. It's strange how the

same person can be so different from his very own
self sometimes.

"Hopper, come back here, show me how to do
all that stuff! I would love to jump in with my
head, like a fancy swimmer, plus those somersaults you just did."

"The somersaults are called turns, when you
finish a lap. And diving just takes practice."

I'm not good at practicing—I get impatient—so I decide to skip practicing and just do the diving itself. I get out of the pool and stand in the same position Hopper did. It doesn't look that hard. You just aim your head down and jump forward in a big curve—what could go wrong?

I reach out my arms, I bend my knees, and then, as big as I can, I JUMP. . . .

Eighteen

Hopper

The slapping sound of Quinny's belly flop echoes through the whole pool.

It makes my own belly sting.

I swim over to her. She flails and splashes and coughs.

I pull her over to the side of the pool. She's coughing even more now.

"Quinny, are you okay?"

Dad swims over to us. The lifeguard comes over, too.

"I'm great!" She coughs. "Super-duper! But Hopper, jumping in with your head first is harder than it looks. Why didn't you tell me?"

"It's okay. Just breathe."

Dad and the lifeguard go away after Quinny calms down a bit. Her mom is busy talking to a grown-up by the locker rooms and I guess didn't even see her do the belly flop. I stay with Quinny. I want to make sure she's really okay. We dangle our feet in the pool. Sitting here with her feels more important than swimming by myself.

"Sorry," says Quinny. "You can go back in and swim."

"I don't mind. Does it still hurt? I know belly flops really hurt."

"A little. I don't think I can feel my belly, actually. Hopper, by the way, how did you sneak under the water so fast and slippery?"

"What do you mean?"

"It's like you just disappeared all quiet without even letting anyone know."

"I don't know. I swim a lot, I guess. Grandpa Gooley used to take me a lot."

"Not me." She looks down. "I guess I'm not a very good swimmer."

I look down, too. Her feet in the water look pizza-dough pale, while mine are almost the color of a walnut. "You have a lot of potential," I tell her. "A lot of energy and enthusiasm."

Quinny smiles. Finally, she seems ready to get back in the water.

"Wait here a minute." I get up. "Stay right here, don't move."

I rush back to the locker room and find my bag. I get out my old goggles, the ones I don't wear anymore because Dad got me these fancy new blue ones for my birthday.

I go back out to Quinny, and pull my blue goggles off, and hand them to her.

"Really?" She smiles. "Wow, thanks, Hopper."

I put on my old brown goggles while she stretches the new blue ones over her head.

These old goggles make me feel good. They remind me of Grandpa Gooley, who used to take me to Open Swim. But then last month Dad started taking me, and he got me the fancy new goggles, and it all seemed to make him really happy—coming to the pool with me, swimming laps, doing something together. Dad even has a picture of me and him in his office, both of us wearing the new blue goggles. It's okay with me, I guess. But sometimes I miss just going swimming with Grandpa Gooley, who didn't get so excited about it all.

"Whoa," says Quinny, looking through those blue goggles for the first time. They turn the whole world blue and a little bit clearer, so you have to get used to them.

"Let's start at the beginning," I say. "The freestyle is the most basic swimming stroke."

I show her how to do the freestyle. Then she does it, but not like how I showed her.

She flaps one arm up and over, and digs beneath the water with the other arm, way too fast. Her legs pop up in a big splash every once in a while, and she's sticking her tongue out.

"Slow down, Quinny . . . what's the rush?"

"Can we work on diving?" she asks. "Or somersaults?"

"We need to work on your basic freestyle technique first."

"Or cannonballs! I think we need to work on my basic cannonball technique!"

"We can do cannonballs after you swim freestyle from here to the edge of the pool."

I show her the right freestyle positions again. Where your head and arms should be. How to turn your head to the side while you swim, so you can breathe.

She does a lopsided Quinny-paddle again.

I don't think she'll ever be an Olympic swimmer, but after a few more tries her Quinny-paddle starts to look a little stronger, a little smoother. It's turning into a freestyle, Quinny-style.

"Hopper, this is hard—how did you get to be such an amazing swimmer?"

"Grandpa Gooley taught me. He can teach you to swim, too, when he gets back."

"Or you could. You're already doing it, right now."

I kind of am. If only she would pay attention.

Quinny's mom comes over and watches us and waves.

"Mom, look, Hopper reminded me how to swim! Now we're working on cannonballs!"

Quinny pulls me over to the side of the pool.

We climb out and jump back in—both of us at once, her hand grabbing on to mine. We explode down into the water.

Quinny waves to me underwater. Her body twists sideways and upside down. Her hair pokes out from her swim cap and floats gently, like reddish seaweed. Her cheeks puff out and her blue-goggle eyes are an even brighter blue.

It's quiet under the water. Life feels slower and gentler down here.

I appreciate it while it lasts.

Back home, Quinny runs off to see the chickens, but her mom stays in our driveway and thanks me for helping her swim. She offers me a five-dollar bill. Wow.

But I don't take the money—she doesn't have to pay me to be with Quinny.

Mrs. Bumble slips it into my bag anyway. She says her family is going to join the Y. She asks if I could give Quinny another "swimming lesson" sometime.

I can't believe she said lesson. Like I'm a real teacher.

I say yes. She smiles and says, "I'm glad you guys are friends."

I'm glad, too. I wave good-bye and head inside.

I think about what to do with my new five-dollar bill.

To: sramsey@wves.edu
From: carolinegrey@zmail.com
Saturday, Nov 22; 11:43 a.m.

Principal Ramsey,

This is Hopper Grey typing again.

Thank you for letting me turn the Friendship Bench into the Books & Buddies Bench. Caleb and I are still painting it. Xander is helping, and Juniper a little, too. I think it looks pretty good so far. The wagon full of books is out there, too. But the problem is those books will get ruined if we leave them outside all the time.

So here is another idea. I want to make a Little Free Library to go with the bench. It is a small house to keep the books dry and safe. It's like a chicken coop for books. Anyone can borrow books from it, or even keep the books. You trust people to use it and take books out and put books in. The first Little Free Library was built in 2009 in Hudson, Wisconsin. Now there are more than fifty thousand of them all over the world. I did not make this up. I looked it up on my mom's computer. The website LittleFreeLibrary.org has more information.

I hope you say yes, because I'm already saving money to buy wood to make a Little Free Library. I'm going to run the Turkey Trot race with Mom next week to raise money. I'm also getting paid money to give Quinny Bumble swimming lessons. I just got five dollars for doing that today. Quinny will need a lot of lessons, since she likes to spend all her time doing cannonballs.

Please let me know if you think the Little Free Library is a good idea. I could start as soon as I have enough money saved up to buy the wood.

Your student,
Hopper Grey

Nineteen

Quinny

After almost a week of asking for autographs, my *save the cookies!* petition is finally impressive enough to show Principal Ramsey.

I see him in the hall on Tuesday morning talking to Nurse Mira, and pull out my petition.

"Look, Principal Ramsey, I have almost a hundred autographs, would you like to sign it, too?"

He makes a *very funny* smile and takes a peek at the petition—and then he looks concerned. "Hmm. Quinny, I think we need to talk."

"Sure. I'm free right now!"

Principal Ramsey guides me to a corner of the hallway. "Quinny, the problem I'm seeing, apart from how messy this is, is that a student petition needs to be signed by students—"

"Oh, it is signed by students!"

"I meant signed *only* by students—that's a student council rule. Also, you need first and last names, printed, and with homerooms or grades, so we know who everyone is."

"But I do know who everyone is—I met every single person who signed this."

"I'm sorry, Quinny, those are the rules. First names and last."

Ugh. Hopper did say something about that before, but I didn't really listen. I can't believe this. It took me tons of days just to get all these autographs and now they don't even count?

After Principal Ramsey finishes picking on my petition, I spend lunch and recess feeling slumpy and stuck. There is nothing worse than having to do a whole bunch of work all over again because you did it wrong the first time.

Then it's time for math and I'm still so upset that I can't focus on the quiz Mrs. Flavio gives us. I don't know the answers, so I just doodle on that quiz. Everyone is writing down numbers, but I draw a cookie. I curve my hand around that doodle so nobody can see that I'm not answering a real math question.

After the quiz, Mrs. Flavio talks and writes on the whiteboard, and I don't understand the new math stuff she says there, either. Then she hands us back our math homework from yesterday and puts mine facedown on my desk.

I understand what *that* means. Everybody does.

After math, it's time to walk to art, but Mrs. Flavio stops me.

"Quinny? I need a word with you. . . ."

Whenever Mrs. Flavio says that, it's never just one word that she needs.

She pulls me to her desk and her face looks at me, all strict, but then her voice is kind of gentle. "I know math has been a struggle lately. I've spoken to your parents, and we agree that we need to get you some extra support."

Not again! Earlier this fall Mrs. Flavio already talked to my parents about how I'm bad at being a normal person in her class. Now she told them I'm bad at math, too?

"Mrs. Flavio, I promise I'll get better at math, you didn't have to tell my parents—"

"You're not in trouble, Quinny. Ms. Jasani and I have some ideas for how to help you."

I've never met Ms. Jasani, but I know who she is, because she always smiles at everyone in the hall. She's not the boss of her own classroom, exactly, but she's got this room down by the cafeteria called Math Lounge. I think she gets stuck with all the dummies. I can't believe I'm actually one of them now.

I don't even remember what happens in art. That's how bad I'm feeling.

Luckily, school is over right after art. I go to my locker to get ready for dismissal, and that's when I see a folded piece of paper on the floor, right in front of it.

I pick that paper up, because littering is not okay, and I notice that it says SMART LIST at the top. And then it lists the names of everyone in our class.

Victoria's name is in the number one spot.

And guess whose name is in the last spot?

I can't even breathe.

I look at my name at the very bottom of that very, very, extra-very awful list.

Then I look over at Victoria. Because this list is in her very own handwriting.

"What's that?" Kaitlin looks over my shoulder.

I try to move the paper away, but she takes it from me.

Kaitlin looks at it with McKayla. Other kids come and look, too. I reach for it but can't get it back. People look confused, some of them giggle, some of them look shocked.

I walk over to Victoria. "Why did you give me that mean list?"

"What?" She sees people looking at it now, too. She looks panicky. "But I didn't."

"It's your writing!"

Victoria shakes her head. She looks really confused.

I'm not confused at all. I know for sure that I hate Victoria Porridge.

"Quinny, where did you get that?" Her voice is all trembly.

"From you. Because you wrote that awful thing."

"But I . . . that's not . . . I didn't even . . ."
Victoria can't get her words out. And there is a
look on her face that I've never seen there before—
an embarrassed, guilty, helpless look.

Some boys are looking at that list now. They're
laughing. They're looking at me.

It's official. I'm the dumbest dodo-head of my
whole class, and everyone knows it.

Mrs. Flavio comes over to remind us to line
up for dismissal, but no one is paying attention to
her because everyone is passing that Smart List
around, and whispering and pointing and laughing at the dummy at the bottom of the list (me).

And then Alex (number ten on the list—not
bad) figures out that my last name, Bumble,
rhymes with Dumble. He shares this information
with the whole entire world.

Quinny Dumble.

I suck in a sniffle and it burns the back of my
throat. I wish I had a better brain that was good
at math and school and all that brainy classroom
stuff. But I'm always in trouble for having my
personality, for just being alive in my own way,
and now for not understanding decimals when the

entire rest of the class thinks they're easy. I can't wait until I get home, so I can cry for real. But if you're stuck at school, crying in the bathroom is the next best thing to crying at home, so I run off to that bathroom.

And I don't even stop when Mrs. Flavio calls after me.

Hopper

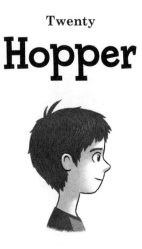

I was afraid this would happen.

I should have ripped up that stupid Smart List when I had the chance, back when Kaitlin showed it to me on the Friendship Bench last week.

Now it's out in the open, and everyone is looking at it and going berserk.

Quinny's face is red and crumpled. Victoria looks confused and shocked. Kaitlin is making a big, surprised fuss with a bunch of other kids by the lockers. She's acting like she has never seen that Smart List before. Something's not right about that.

I try to get Quinny's attention, but she turns and runs.

I go after her. It's my job to help her feel better. That's what friends do.

But I'm not allowed into the girls' bathroom.

Nurse Mira is, though. She shows up a few moments later and sends me back to Mrs. Flavio, who makes us all get back in line for dismissal.

I follow the bussers outside and on board, like always. I sit in my seat and wait for Quinny to come sit next to me. The bus fills up with kids and growls to a start. Quinny gets on at the last minute. Her face is all blotchy and puffy, and her eyes won't look at me.

She sits right up front, next to Darla the bus aide.

If she were sitting next to me, I would pull out my neon-green juggling sacs and toss them up into a three-ball cascade. (I don't like juggling in public, but I'd make an exception for Quinny.) I would tell her she has twenty thousand hairs inside each of her ears, and so does everyone. I would remind her that Victoria doesn't get to decide who is smart. I would talk about the new chickens and distract Quinny from her feelings, and she would forget to be sad.

But I can't do any of that, because she sat up front.

When the bus finally gets to our stop, Quinny gets off ahead of me and walks away.

"Quinny, wait—let's go see the chickens," I call out.

"I've got soccer," she mumbles, and keeps walking.

She doesn't have soccer until four. That's also when my brothers go, straight from middle school. "You have a few minutes until you have to leave," I tell her.

Quinny whips her head around and shoots back a teary glare and steps toward me. "You knew I was dumb this whole time and you didn't even tell me?!"

I back up a little. "Quinny, you're not dumb."

"I'm not going to the chickens and I'm not going back to school ever again. My cookie petition is all wrong and I flunked my decimals quiz and everybody was laughing because I am at the bottom of the list and they were all laughing and pointing and . . ."

Quinny gulps some air and hiccups. I wish I

could hand her a glass of water. I wish I could make her see the truth: that everyone at school seemed mostly shocked and upset at Victoria. I don't think they were really making fun of Quinny.

She takes off again before I can figure out how to say this.

"Hopper, what happened at school?" says Quinny's dad.

I tell him about the Smart List. I tell him about the awful name Alex called Quinny. The more I tell him, the more he groans and rubs the back of his neck.

"Thanks for telling me," he says. "I'll talk to her once she's calmed down and we'll work this out with the school. But for now, let's just give her some space."

We don't really have much choice, since she just ran off.

I go to the Chalet des Poulets by myself. I fill up the spray bottle and sit with Pumpkin. When she tries to peck me, I spray her in between the eyes. One of these days, she'll learn.

Poodle hops down from the rafters, brave enough to limp closer now that I'm here to protect her from Pumpkin. Polar Bear won't come out of the henhouse. None of them have laid any eggs yet. They're all still kind of shocked to be here, I guess.

I spot something moving by the door. It's not a squirrel or a predator, it's Piper.

Piper has a mini-Quinny face, but her personality is different. She likes to sneak and lurk and hide—once Quinny and I even caught her spying on us from up in Mrs. Porridge's fig tree.

Piper creeps into the Chalet des Poulets now and tucks herself in a corner.

"How's Quinny?" I ask her.

She *shhh*es me with a finger. Her dad comes by a moment later, with her backpack. He looks tired.

"How's Quinny?" I ask him.

"She ate some pie and left for soccer. And I left a message for Principal Ramsey," he says. "Piper, I know you're in there. You can't just run off like that."

Piper peeks out at him. "Hopper needs help with the chickens," she says.

I look at Piper and then at her dad. "I need help with the chickens," I say.

"Sweetie, you need to do your language-arts homework," he says. "C'mon now."

This is not the first time I've seen Piper hiding from her homework.

"Mr. Bumble, let her stay and do it here with me. I'll bring her back right after."

Mr. Bumble looks at me like I just offered him a million dollars.

I know Piper is having trouble learning her letters and doing her worksheets. I've heard Mr. Bumble complaining about this to Mom at the bus stop.

"She's all yours, Hopper," he says. "Good luck."

He hands me her homework and a pencil, and he bolts. Okay. I never had these kinds of worksheets in kindergarten. They look easy (for me) and boring (for Piper). I get that she has to learn her letters, so she can learn words, so she can learn sentences and paragraphs and eventually learn how to read books. I get that. She has to start at the beginning.

Unless, of course, she starts at the end, where it's actually interesting. With a book, itself.

"Piper, wait here, I'll be right back." I get up. "Just stay right here and spray Pumpkin between the eyes if she tries to peck at you, okay?"

Piper looks excited and takes the water bottle. I run back home and upstairs to my room.

Here is what I know: Piper likes chess, numbers, trees, chickens, worms, and pretty much anything gross. She doesn't like language-arts worksheets, but she loves it when people read *to* her. She's good at memorizing things. She already knows her times tables better than Quinny.

I go to my closet. I pick out some big picture books. I don't have any books on chickens, but there's one on poop—close enough, since chickens make a lot of it.

I bring a pile of books out to the Chalet des Poulets.

And that's when I see Pumpkin pecking away at Piper's language-arts worksheet, like it's the most delicious worksheet she's ever tasted.

"Pumpkin, no!" I call out. "Piper, spray her with the bottle. What are you doing?"

"She's letting the chicken eat her homework, obviously," answers Mrs. Porridge, watching from her back porch. "Good riddance, if you ask me."

"Your dad will be mad. You're supposed to *do* your homework, not feed it to a chicken."

"I'm perfectly happy to take the blame," says Mrs. Porridge. "Or the credit."

"Look, I brought some stories." I show her the books. "Which one should we read?"

Piper looks reluctant.

"Polar Bear still seems worried and scared to be here," I say to her. "If you read to someone, it helps them feel better. Let's try, okay?"

I open a book—*Peanut Butter and Brains*. Piper pretends to gag, but stays close to me.

I read out loud to the chickens. I do the voices, just like Ms. Yoon used to do at school before she left to have her baby. Polar Bear pops her head out of the henhouse. Poodle watches us through her poufy bangs. Walter and Cha-Cha lounge by a tree, paying attention.

Even Pumpkin, still chewing bits of Piper's homework, settles in to listen.

Everyone is looking at me reading out loud. Piper giggles. The chickens *bock* and *bip*. I usually don't like being the center of attention, but this time it feels okay since I'm just saying the book's words, not my own words.

When I'm done reading, Piper claps. She hands me another book—*The Snurtch*.

This time, I try something different. I read a page out loud, and then I ask Piper to read that same page out loud with me. I point to each word as we say it together.

Polar Bear lingers in the henhouse doorway.

Poodle hops closer and stares at us harder, as we read.

Pumpkin, finally done with her homework

snack, cozies up to Piper's side and *bip-burps.*

Walter has fallen asleep, with Cha-Cha relaxing on top of him.

Piper leans against me as we keep turning the pages and reading out loud.

I don't know if this is the right way to teach a person how to read. (I can't even remember how I learned, it was such a long time ago.) But I do know . . . I never had to do all those worksheets in kindergarten. And I still learned how to read, somehow.

I'm almost done reading the second book with Piper when Mom walks over to the Chalet des Poulets. She's wearing her running stuff. She listens to me and Piper finish the book.

"Wow, guys, that was terrific. Hopper, I'm going for a run. Want to come along?"

Piper looks disappointed.

"I'll keep reading with her, you go." Mrs. Porridge nods at me, like she's happy for once.

Now would be a good time to ask Mrs. Porridge to sponsor me for the Turkey Trot and help raise money for the Little Free Library. The race is in just a couple of days. I've e-mailed my relatives and all my parents' friends. But I have a hard time asking people face-to-face.

I open my mouth and try to say a sentence about the race to Mrs. Porridge.

But I chicken out.

Mom and I go for a run.

I notice it's easier for me to talk while I'm running than while I'm standing still. Maybe pounding my feet on the ground shakes loose more words from my brain.

I tell Mom how I was trying to help Piper with her reading, and also help the chickens.

"It didn't look like you were trying," she says. "It looked like you were succeeding."

I tell her what happened at school today with Quinny and the Smart List.

"Oh, that's terrible," she says. "Kids can be so cruel. That Victoria is such a puzzle."

Victoria *is* a puzzle. She looked just as surprised and upset as Quinny did to see that Smart List, even though she's the one who wrote it. Kaitlin is kind of a puzzle, too. She pretended she'd never seen that Smart List before, even though she showed it to me last week.

"Well, I'm glad Quinny has a kind, thoughtful friend like you," says Mom. "She's an awesome kid with so many great qualities. I bet you'll find a way to cheer her up."

I bet I will, too. I just can't think of one right now.

"Hopper, slow down." Mom gets out of breath.

I don't want to slow down. I'm not even running as fast as I can—I've been going slower just so I can stay with Mom. I'm excited to train for the Turkey Trot, and not just because it will help raise money for the Little Free Library. I also want to see who wins the race. It might even be me, if I run fast enough. Normally I don't care about winning, but this time feels different.

"Go too fast and you'll burn out in the end," says Mom. "You need to pace yourself."

"But I still have lots of energy."

"Sweetie, all runners have to learn to pace themselves. Sometimes the fastest way to get where you're going is to . . . slow down."

Okay. Fine. I slow down. Even though I don't want to.

"Now, there's something I need to tell you," she says. "It's not great news, I'm afraid. . . ."

That's when Mom says I can't run the Turkey Trot. You have to be *ages twelve and up* to get an official race number and T-shirt. I won't be able to win, even if I'm the fastest one.

"Sorry, Hopper. I should've looked up the rules. But we can still keep running together for fun, and I'll share half the money from my sponsors with you for the Little Free Library, okay?"

I nod. That definitely cheers me up.

When we're almost done running, I think of a way to cheer Quinny up, too.

It's something we only do on special occasions. But helping a friend feel better is special enough, I think. I look up at Mom. I try to remember what's inside our fridge.

"Mom, do we have any pickles?"

Twenty-one

Quinny

The best thing about being at soccer is that no one here knows about that Smart List.

My brain may not be all that brainy, but my feet feel pretty smart bossing that ball around. I kick and run and dodge and twist past everyone. I bang myself into anyone who comes too close. I am fierce and fast and I am ONE WITH THE BALL.

That is something Trevor and Ty like to say. And now I like to say it, too.

But then Alex Delgado shows up, to do a makeup practice.

"Look who's here, Quinny Dumble!"

Great, my new nickname. Before it was Big

Mouth. Then it turned into Big Foot, since I'm such a ferocious kicker. Now Alex changed it again. But who even gave him the right?

I know it's not okay to kick a person (like Alex) in the shins in regular life. But if he gets in my way when I'm kicking a soccer ball, that's not my fault, is it? And there's no rule against picturing Alex's face on the ball I'm about to kick, right?

THWWWAAACK!!

I'm super tired after soccer. I used every single muscle inside me and now I'm just a limp noodle. Ty and Trevor thumb-wrestle on the way home, but I remember the bad stuff from school and close my eyes as Mr. Grey drives. When he turns onto our block we slow down, which jolts me awake, and I see Hopper sitting on my front steps. He stands up when he sees me.

I thank Mr. Grey and walk up my driveway toward our back door.

"Quinny, wait." Hopper walks after me. "I have a surprise for you."

That's not fair—he knows I can't resist surprises.

"Fine, what is it? But make it quick because I just want to go inside and be slumpy."

Hopper leads me back to his house, and into his kitchen, where the table is set for a MAKE YOUR OWN PIZZA PARTY with a gazillion bowls of toppings and balls of squishy dough and fluffs of flour and plates and a big jug of strawberry lemonade, which Mom never lets me have because I'm already too hyper. One of those toppings bowls is full of pickles. Another is full of crumbled bits of bacon. Pickles and bacon are my two favorite things about having a tongue. (Coconut snowball cookies are a close number three.)

Hopper had a different pizza party earlier this fall, but I missed that pizza party (long story), so now is my chance! I squish the dough and spoon sauce onto it and load my pizza with yellow cheese and white cheese and green peppers and red peppers and mushrooms and olives and of course bacon. I save the pickles for when the pizza is already cooked.

"Wait—Hopper, you know what would make this pizza party even more perfect?"

"Uh, no."

"Wait here, I'll be right back!"

I come back to the pizza party with Crescent in his little guinea-pig pouch.

"Mrs. Grey, can I borrow some red peppers? They're Crescent's favorite veggie."

"Sure thing, Quinny, but we have a house rule—no rodents at the kitchen table."

That's not a fair rule if you ask me, but I mind my manners.

"Sorry, Mrs. Grey, I forgot to ask if Crescent was invited to the pizza party."

"Apology accepted," she says.

"Let's do a pizza picnic in the hall," says Hopper.

Oh, that boy is full of good ideas! We spread a beach towel in the hall, which makes me think of summer, even though it's November. I sniff that towel. The beautiful smell of chlorine reminds me I want to go swimming again. (I definitely need to work on my cannonball.)

The pizza comes out of the oven all bubbly and crispy, and I chomp a big bite. I give Crescent some crust and his blurry little mouth does some super-speedy munching.

"Quinny, take it easy, you don't want to choke," says Hopper.

I take a breath and chew more carefully. My tummy feels so happy and relaxed.

But then, when my plate is finally empty, it hits me: the pizza is all gone, but my math homework is still all there, waiting in my backpack.

"Well, thanks for the pizza," I tell Hopper. "But I better go home and do some math since I'm such a dummy at school."

"Quinny, stop saying that, you're not dumb."

"Tell that to the quiz I flunked. And did you know I have to start going to Ms. Jasani in Math Lounge?"

"So? Lots of people go there. Ms. Jasani is really nice."

Daddy said going to Math Lounge will be good for me. He said it'll be like my own private math class. But who in the world would ever want their own private math class?

"It doesn't matter anyway, because my report card will still be full of F-minuses."

"There's no such thing as an F-minus," says Hopper. "And report cards won't come out for a long time. You don't know what your grades will be."

"Yes, I do. School is always hard for me and my report card is never too fantastic."

I didn't ever tell Hopper that before, because I didn't want him to think I was a big giant dodohead. I'm wobbly at math, but even at reading I'm not so hot. I'm a fantastic reader when it comes to picture books, of course—I read those out loud to my little sisters a lot, or at least I used to before I started doing so much soccer—but the problem is that thicker books without pictures make me hungry by the time I get to page eight or nine. Even if there's no food in the book! It's the weirdest thing. And, believe me, third grade has tons more thicker books without pictures. Plus, math that's so fast and so confusing, it might as well be a magic trick. The teachers want us to keep getting smarter and smarter, until our heads explode, I guess.

"Maybe the problem isn't you—maybe it's the report card," says Hopper.

"I know, I wish I could just burn that thing up before my parents see it."

"No, I mean, report cards aren't the only way of

being smart. You do stuff every day you're smart at, Quinny. Like being kind, funny, and nice. That stuff isn't on a report card."

I roll my eyes at him. "Because those things don't count."

"Of course they count. Smart is . . . like pizza toppings. There's lots of different flavors. Don't you see? You're smart at being with people—everyone wants to talk to you, and play with you, and be your partner for projects. You make the pizza more delicious."

That's a lot of words Hopper just said. But they don't make much sense to me.

"Hopper, thank you for saying I'm delicious, but school doesn't really care about pizza, or being friendly—they care about grades and homework and quizzes."

"I can help you with your homework."

"Not now. I'm tired from soccer."

Plus, from eating a whole pizza with six toppings. Crescent helped, but not much.

I rub his little ears in his pouch, and then we get up. "Say bye, Crescent. Say thank you."

"Wait, there's dessert." Hopper gets up, too. "Mom made lemon bars."

"Lemon bars?" I slump against the wall. "Oh no, Hopper, why did you just tell me that? Don't you remember the lemon bars that Izzy brought in for her birthday last month? They were delicious. But that's never going to happen again, because my petition to save the cookies is a big giant failure, too—"

"Quinny—"

"Good-bye. I'm going home now to be sad under my covers."

"Quinny, wait—what if . . ."

Hopper walks across the hall and picks up a book sitting on a table. It's the book we made together last month about his tonsils surgery. I don't know why he's staring at it now.

"What if I know a way to get Principal Ramsey to change the food rules?" he says.

"What?" I laugh at him. "No way."

"I'm serious. Go get that petition, and I'll show you."

Twenty-two

Hopper

I stare at the tonsils book, with my name and Quinny's name on the cover.

"What if I know a way to get Principal Ramsey to change the food rules?"

Quinny laughs. She doesn't think I'm being serious.

But I've known Principal Ramsey a long time. If we take all the whining out of the petition and add in a compromise, I bet he'll change the rules.

"We need to think of a compromise." I hold up the tonsils book.

"Hopper, that sounds like an awful word, whatever it means. And why are you holding up

150

our tonsils book? It's a fabulous book, but it has nothing to do with cookies or petitions."

"You remember how we both wanted our names to go first on this cover? So we talked about it and decided that my name would go first, because they were my tonsils that were getting taken out, but your name would be bigger, because a lot of the ideas in the book came from you. That's a compromise. We could ask Principal Ramsey to change the food rules a little so you get some of what you want, but he still gets some of what he wants."

"But Hopper, I want *everything* I want! That's why I made the petition."

"Get real, Quinny, he's not going to say okay, bring back all the cookies, just like that. If you don't offer a compromise, he won't take you seriously, no matter how many kids sign their names. And the petition also needs to be shorter and calmer. We need to revise it."

Ms. Yoon talked to us about revising before she left school to have her baby. Revising means making sure your spelling and grammar are correct. It also means finding a better and clearer way to say what you're trying to say, and improving the ideas behind your words.

"Revising? Snore," says Quinny. "The words in my petition are already fantastic."

"Pretend you're Principal Ramsey. Would you rather read a long petition full of cranky words, whining the same thing over and over, or a short, calm one that offers a compromise?"

Quinny doesn't say. I can tell she knows the answer but doesn't want to admit it.

Then I suggest a compromise that she can suggest in her petition.

Quinny crosses her arms over her chest, but she listens.

Her face gets softer as I talk. And then she starts bouncing a little.

"Okay, Hopper, maybe you're right . . . it's worth a try, let's go get that petition and calm it down with your compromise."

We go over to Quinny's house. But Cleo is screaming for her Binky again, so we come back to my house, where it's quieter. We go up to my parents' room. Quinny talks, and I talk, and then

I type the best parts of all our talking onto Mom's computer:

Dear Principal Ramsey,

This is a letter about the new rules that get rid of cookies and sweets from hot lunch and classroom parties. We disagree with the rules, because sweets add a lot of fun and happiness to school. We know it is important to be healthy and we understand if you have to take the dessert out of hot lunch. It doesn't always taste so great anyway. But here is a different idea that still lets us have some fun in school, but also has less sugar. This idea is called a compromise:

1) Can you please let us have sweets once a month for a group birthday celebration in our class? So we'll still get to have birthdays, but there will be fewer cupcakes and cookies total.

2) Can you please still let us bring treats for the winter holiday party? A holiday party without holiday cookies is a very dull party. For Halloween we get candy from trick-or-treating, so we don't need sweets in school as much, but for the winter holiday party, we would really miss those cookies. And you could make a big rule that says none of the cookies that people bring in can ever have tree nuts or peanuts in them. (Or even dairy, if you want.)

We think this compromise is a smart way to keep us

healthy and also keep us happy. Please let us know what you think. We are free to talk anytime. Especially Quinny, who started this petition in the first place.

Sincerely,

Full name	grade	homeroom
1) Quinny Bumble	3	Mrs. Flavio
2) Hopper Grey	3	Mrs. Flavio
3)		
4)		

Quinny looks at the new petition and then she turns to me, her eyes all wide.

"Oh, Hopper!"

She wraps a hug around me and I freeze. This is the third hug Quinny has ever given me and, as usual, it's too tight. The only good thing about it is that her hair smells like peaches (from her shampoo, I guess). I hold still, with my arms stuck to my sides. I'm relieved when Quinny finally lets me go.

"Principal Ramsey is for sure going to love this super-brainy and very, very, extra-very polite petition!" she says. "All we need now is a bunch more autographs on it. And can you draw some cookies on it, again? Wait, wait! Can you draw a picture of *kids doing homework while eating cookies*? Because cookies make it easier to do homework, and homework makes you smarter, so cookies for sure make you smarter."

Quinny might be surprised to hear this, but I don't think homework makes you smarter.

I think helping people and solving problems and finding something to feel curious about makes you smarter. I think making stuff, and making stuff up, definitely makes me feel smarter.

I'm happy that I'm helping Quinny. Even if I have to get hugged for it.

"Hopper, this beautiful new petition calls for a celebration." She drags me back down to the kitchen. "Let's eat some of those amazing, delicious lemon bars right this minute."

Quinny is so cheered up that she eats three lemon bars. Meanwhile I get my charcoal pencils and draw some kids eating cookies while doing homework on the revised petition. I don't think it'll make a big difference to Principal Ramsey, but you never know.

"Hopper, thank you for being the smartest cookie ever." Quinny's smile is full of crumbs. "What would I do without your talented charcoal pencils and your big, giant brain?"

It's nice that Quinny thinks I'm so brainy, but it also bothers me a little. She's still acting like smart is something that belongs just to me.

After she goes home, I go back upstairs to my room and get out my sketch pad.

There's got to be a way for me to show her how smart she really is.

Twenty-three

Quinny

It's the day before Thanksgiving and I'm thankful Victoria is not by the lockers. But I also want to see her, because I have a million questions about why she's such an awful friend.

In class, we're supposed to start the day with morning meeting, but instead Principal Ramsey comes in with a big important look on his face. And, wow, Victoria and Alex come in with him, and they scurry over to their seats. Victoria looks dazed and kind of queasy. Alex is making that face where you try to pretend that something big isn't a big deal.

"Kids, Mrs. Flavio, good morning everyone . . . settle down now, I'd like to have a few words, in light of a certain piece of paper that made the rounds yesterday afternoon."

Principal Ramsey tells us he knows about the Smart List, and that it was hurtful and dishonest, because "you are all bright, capable students" and he reminds us we have a no-bullying rule at school. While he talks all his grown-up talking, Victoria slouches in her seat. Principal Ramsey doesn't say her name, but everyone can tell who he's talking about. I see other kids glare at Victoria, and I'm glad, because she deserves all the glares in the world.

After Principal Ramsey leaves, Mrs. Flavio says, "And that's the end of that. Onward!"

We zip through morning meeting and then we have ELA, which I like because it's made up of words, not numbers. Today, since it's early dismissal, Mrs. Flavio reads an out-loud story instead of making us do our own reading or writing. I'm excited, because I like out-loud stories more than flat stories on paper. Listening to a story is also MUCH better than writing, because you don't have to think about spelling or grammar, and you don't get graded—you can just relax and listen.

(And I love out-loud stories with pictures the best, because looking at pictures during a story feels more like you're *doing* something.)

After ELA it's time for math, which I don't like since it's made up of gobbledygook. But it turns out that I don't even stay for math, because Mrs. Flavio sends me over to Ms. Jasani, who lives in a smaller room down the hall. And that's called the Math Lounge.

"Quinny, welcome," says Ms. Jasani, who is one of the shortest and most colorful grown-ups in the whole school. "I'm your support teacher for Math Lounge. I'm so happy to meet you."

I don't say anything, because telling her I'm happy to meet her, too, would be a lie.

Here's the truth about Math Lounge: it's where the dummies go if they can't understand a normal math lesson. But I'm surprised to see Darren and So-Mai in here, at a table in the back. They're fourth graders from my bus. They're not dumb—they're friendly and funny—so why are they here? One of them, So-Mai, even won the STOMP award last month. (STOMP stands for

159

student-of-the-month-prize and Principal Ramsey is very picky about who he gives it to.)

"Take a seat, Quinny," says Ms. Jasani. "Or have a ball, if you prefer."

She rolls out a big blue bouncy ball from under the table! And I get to sit on that ball instead of a boring old chair. I wish we had these in my classroom.

"Ms. Jasani, thanks for the fantastic sitty ball, but don't get your hopes up. I can't do decimals, I don't care about sticker rewards, and I don't even like numbers in the first place."

I share all of this awful information, but she doesn't look horrified.

"Understood, Quinny. We'll take it one step at a time. Tiny step by tiny step, together."

"But you don't get it—the smartest girl in my class just made a list that said I was the dumbest kid in my class, so you really don't have a chance."

Ms. Jasani rests her chin on her hand and smiles, all sad and curious. "You know what I think, Quinny? The smartest person in your class would never make a list calling herself the smartest person. Part of being smart is being humble and kind. Now, let's get started."

Actually Ms. Jasani is wrong. Being humble doesn't help you much with math and grades and quizzes. But okay, she sits down with me and we go over decimals from the very beginning, like from when Mrs. Flavio started talking about math back in September.

"Quinny, what do you already know about numbers?"

"Not much, that's why I'm here, I guess."

"Well, what are numbers, anyway? And fractions and decimals . . . ?"

"Numbers are . . . annoying things I have to memorize or I'll flunk out of school. And fractions are numbers in a bunk bed. And decimals . . . have something to do with fractions."

"All right. Did you know that numbers are really just pencils, or socks or . . . cookies?" Ms. Jasani pulls out a chocolate chip cookie—only it's made of paper. "Numbers are symbols that represent something else. Whole numbers are like whole cookies. Here's the number one."

She holds up a paper cookie.

Then she spreads out a bunch more paper cookies and counts from one to ten. I guess I know this stuff already, but the way Ms. Jasani is talking about it now makes it feel . . . less scary.

Then she shows me how to turn those cookies into fractions, by folding each cookie in half, and then in half again.

Then she shows me how to turn those cookies into decimals, by drawing lines on each cookie that splits it into ten slices. So one whole cookie is ten out of ten slices, or 10/10, or 1.0. And each slice is one out of the ten slices that make up a whole cookie, or 1/10, or .10.

I feel like my brain is starting to melt a little now.

But Ms. Jasani explains everything all slow and gentle. And boy, does she like to repeat herself! She doesn't make me nervous, so I can actually hear what she is saying. (Sometimes when I'm nervous my ears don't work too well.) I still don't *understand* every single thing she's saying, but I don't feel as weird about not understanding it. I realize I'm not afraid of Ms. Jasani the way I am of Mrs. Flavio.

Then she pulls out my math quiz from yesterday. I got a 61 out of 100. Yikes.

But she says if I help her do a word problem right now, I'll get ten points of extra credit on that quiz, which means my grade will go from a 61 to a 71, which is an amazing grade.

A word problem is like a cross between numbers and words and a horrible riddle.

Words = Yay!

Word problems = Yuck.

"Ms. Jasani, I would love extra credit, but you're barking up the wrong person. I got a 61 on the quiz, remember, so I'm not too good at figuring out real live word problems."

"Quinny, take a look. This word problem is about something I think you'll like. . . ."

Amina walks into a bakery with $4.00 and a growling stomach. She can't decide which cookie to buy: a snickerdoodle ($1.30), a blondie ($1.60), or a black-and-white cookie ($1.10). Does she have enough money to buy all three cookies?

"Oh, I hope so," I answer. "Because it'd be too hard to choose!"

My mouth feels drooly now. I can't believe this word problem is all about cookies.

Math + cookies + extra credit = an offer I can't refuse.

Ms. Jasani and I get to work, figuring out that word problem. We count the whole numbers. We count up all those decimals.

When the bell rings, I'm not done finding the answer. I freeze.

"It's okay, Quinny, take your time . . . tiny step by tiny step, remember? I can give you a late pass if necessary. Take as much time as you need."

Ms. Jasani stays there next to me, and we find that answer together. And the good news is Amina DOES have enough money for all three cookies— exactly enough. I'm so happy for her!

And then Ms. Jasani pulls out a pack of real live cookies, and offers me one, as a reward for doing that word problem.

"Ms. Jasani, you are breaking the law! You can't have cookies in the classroom anymore.

Didn't you hear about Principal Ramsey's strict new rules?"

"If you tattle on me, Quinny, I won't bring you a cookie next time."

She makes a sneaky face, and wow, that is called a threat, I think. A really fantastic one.

"You did a great job paying attention and working hard, Quinny," she says. "See you next time. And good luck with your petition, by the way. Mrs. Flavio told me all about it."

She smiles at me. And it looks like she's telling the truth, not just trying to make me feel better. Either Ms. Jasani is being honest, or she is a very, very, extra-very good actress.

I walk back to my classroom with a bit of extra pep in my step. Because Math Lounge was not awful—and also, because now it's time for lunch and recess.

The best feeling ever is when lunch and recess are about to start—it feels like you're right about to jump out of a plane! (With a parachute on, of course.)

Everyone's by the lockers getting their lunch boxes and chatting. I stop by my locker and I notice something strange going on. All the girls are talking, but none of them are talking to Victoria. They all walk off and leave her behind.

Victoria looks at me. Her mouth twists. "Quinny . . . ?"

I can't believe she thinks I'm going to forgive her for the Smart List, just like that.

I turn away and head to the cafeteria, too, with my new petition. Hopper said he'd help me get some autographs on it today, since we have to start from scratch.

But before I can find him, Kaitlin comes up to me. "Quinny, I love your socks," she says. "Are you still asking people to sign your petition?"

"It's actually a new and improved petition. I'm kind of starting over. . . ."

"Oh, cool. Can I help?"

"Sure, why not."

Kaitlin is being so nice all of a sudden. I didn't realize she was such a sweet person. I thought she mostly cared about nail polish, like Victoria.

(And she's right that my socks today are pretty amazing—they're covered in watermelon slices, to match my barrette.)

Kaitlin and I spend most of lunch getting kids' autographs on the new, calmer petition.

Xander reads the petition and says, "Wow."

Avery tells us it looks "very professional."

Sawyer says, "Quinny, those cookies look almost real."

That's really a compliment for Hopper, since he drew the cookies. But he's not standing here to accept it, so I smile and thank Sawyer.

I don't see Victoria at all in the cafeteria, and I'm relieved.

I don't see Hopper, either, and I'm confused. Where did he go?

Finally I spot him, coming from the hot lunch line, which sometimes takes forever.

I rush over to him. He's holding a tray. "Hopper Hopper Hopper, there you are. Look, Kaitlin and I just got a bunch of autographs."

"I noticed," says Hopper, looking from me to Kaitlin.

"Do you want to help us?"

Hopper shrugs. "Still gotta eat. Looks like you're doing fine on your own."

"Okay, well, meet us outside for recess?"

He doesn't answer.

"Come on, Quinny," says Kaitlin, pulling me along. "Alex hasn't signed it yet. . . ."

At recess, Kaitlin and I keep walking around with the petition, and McKayla follows us, too, now, and we get lots more autographs.

I finally see Victoria out here, and it shocks me for three reasons.

The first shock: she's sitting on the ground. Victoria never sits on the ground because it would get her clothes dirty.

The second shock: she's sitting alone, behind the sycamore tree, like she is hiding. Victoria usually has people surrounding her and acts like a spotlight is shining on her.

The third shock: there are tears on Victoria's face.

I walk over to her. Because I'm fascinated by those tears.

"Quinny . . ." Victoria's voice is just a rough little squeak.

"Let's go ask Izzy to sign the petition," says Kaitlin, pulling me away.

"Yeah," says McKayla, following Kaitlin.

"Quinny . . . please," says Victoria. "I never wanted anyone to see that thing. . . . I never even brought it to school."

I let go of Kaitlin's hand and look at Victoria. "But it was right by my locker."

"I don't know how it . . ." Victoria's face tips down. "I threw it away at home, honest." She sputters her words. "You can't hate me, Quinny, you just can't, please. . . ."

Even more tears dribble out of her eyes now.

"Give me a break," says Kaitlin, trying to pull me away again. "Let's go get more people to sign your petition before the bell rings."

"Yeah," says McKayla.

McKayla is very, very, extra-very talented at following other people around, I guess.

Me, not so much.

I don't know what to do. (Hopper would know, but he's on the other side of the playground, still painting the Books & Buddies Bench.) I try to think. Victoria said she threw that list away at her house. If that's true, then how did it get by my locker, for me to find?

Maybe she's lying.

I guess it doesn't matter. Because Victoria still made that awful meanie list in the first place, and it called me the dumbest dummy of the whole class. And nothing she says now can make up for that. So I finally just let Kaitlin pull me away from her.

And I only peek back once.

Twenty-four
Hopper

I'm almost done painting the Books & Buddies Bench. But it's hard to focus because of what's going on behind the sycamore tree.

Victoria is sitting there, crying.

I see Quinny and Kaitlin and McKayla walk away from her.

This is none of my business. Victoria is not my favorite person.

But she is still a person.

I put down my paintbrush and walk over to her.

I stand close enough for her to notice me.

She does. And she doesn't send me away with her eyes.

"Why did you do it?" I say. "The Smart List."

Victoria's face gets extra pinched. "Leave me alone."

I sit down next to her.

"I just . . . it was just something to help me work harder, and do better and . . ."

But Victoria is already a hard worker and strong student. I don't understand.

"I wasn't even going to show it to anybody, I threw it in my trash at home." Victoria looks at me all intense now. "I don't even know how it got here, I really don't."

"Honest?"

"Honest! I just wanted to . . . I mean I wanted to win STOMP last month, and I wanted to make my dad see . . . I mean, he was away on a trip, and I just wanted to feel like I was . . ."

She kind of breathes out the last word. *Smart.* She drops her head to her knees.

The STOMP award is a really tough award to win—Principal Ramsey gives out only one each month, which is why it stands for Student of the Month Prize.

"Do you really think Quinny is the dumbest person in our class?" I ask her.

Victoria shakes her head. "No way. And I'm not the smartest, either. You are."

"I'm not," I say. "I'm really not. There's no such thing. Everybody is just . . . different."

Victoria looks at me. I've never seen her face so blotchy before.

"I'm sorry I even made that stupid list. I don't even know how it got to school, I swear."

There is something I could say here, about Kaitlin, but I don't say it.

"You've got paint on your shirt," Victoria says next.

I look down at my chest. "I'm almost done with the bench."

"That's outdoor paint. It's tough to get out, but I know how, because I'm an expert on stains and doing laundry."

"Laundry?" I know Victoria wears a lot of complicated clothes. But I didn't know she washes them herself. That surprises me.

"Masha taught me. Laundry has a lot to do with science, you might like it."

I shrug at this.

"Your bench looks nice," she says. "Even

though people don't want to read at recess."

"They might," I say. "If there's a bench to do it on. And books to choose from. After I finish the bench, I'm going to build a Little Free Library. I'm saving up money for that."

I tell Victoria about the Little Free Library project. And she actually listens.

"Hopper?" A voice interrupts me. "What are you doing?"

I look up. It's Quinny.

She, Kaitlin, and McKayla are all staring down at me. I don't know what to say.

"He's being nice to someone who was mean to you," Kaitlin answers for me.

I look at Kaitlin now, right into her eyes. I know she had that Smart List before Quinny found it by her locker. I know she was the one who wanted Quinny to see it.

But I really don't want to get sucked into this. Drama is not my style.

And why should I do something nice for Victoria, when she's never done anything nice for me? I should keep my mouth shut, which is the most comfortable position for it to be in.

And yet . . . Quinny deserves to know the truth.

And the truth deserves to have people know it. So, I take a deep breath.

"Kaitlin showed me that Smart List last week," I tell Quinny. "She's the one who had it."

"What?" Kaitlin's mouth snarls. "Hopper, cut it out."

"She showed it to me at recess. She wanted me to tell you about it."

"I did not!"

Victoria sits up a little and looks at Kaitlin. "You were at my house. For a playdate. You were in my room."

"So? I go to lots of people's houses," says Kaitlin.

"Did you steal that Smart List?" asks Victoria. "I never wanted anyone to see it!"

Kaitlin looks uncomfortable now. "It was trash," she says. "You threw it away."

"So *you* left the Smart List by my locker?" Quinny says to Kaitlin. "You stole it from Victoria's trash and brought it to school, even though you knew it would hurt my feelings?"

"I . . . didn't steal. . . . She threw it out!"

"You should say sorry to Victoria," I tell Kaitlin. "That was her private garbage can."

Kaitlin does not say sorry. She glares a mean face at me.

"And you can't get mad at Hopper for telling," says Quinny. "Because he did an honest thing and you did a sneaky thing."

"Yeah," says McKayla.

"McKayla, please stop agreeing with everybody," says Quinny. "It's driving me nuts. You're your own person, you should figure out your own opinion."

"Victoria thinks you're a dummy," Kaitlin says to Quinny. "She thinks everybody is a dummy but her."

"I do not," Victoria says. Her eyes are full of tears. "I'm the dummy for making that list. I was just trying to make myself feel smarter, and it didn't even work."

"Victoria made a bad mistake," Quinny says to Kaitlin. "But you tried to hurt people's feelings on purpose, which in my opinion I think is worse."

Quinny glares at Kaitlin. Victoria shoots a hurt look at Kaitlin.

Other people are around us, too, now, staring at Kaitlin.

Everyone switches from being mad at Victoria to being mad at Kaitlin.

Kaitlin looks like she's about to cry.

All that drama didn't go away. It's just going around in circles.

Twenty-five

Quinny

All of a sudden the tears switch from Victoria's face to Kaitlin's, and now I have to be mad at Kaitlin, too, I guess. But being mad is hard work, and that's it, I've had enough.

It's the day before Thanksgiving, can't we all just be nice?

Be nice, forgive people, have fun, be grateful, and not be awful?

I'm going to forgive everyone and end all this stupid stuff right now.

"Victoria, guess what, I'll forgive you for making the Smart List, if you forgive Kaitlin for stealing it. And Kaitlin, I'll forgive you for stealing it, if you forgive Hopper for tattling on you.

Not that he did anything wrong, but you know what I mean. Okay? Deal?"

I have everyone's attention now.

"I'm serious, guys, I don't like fights," I say in my biggest voice. "I don't like whispers and glares and gossip and hurt feelings . . . plus it's Thanksgiving, so we should be thankful and kind and mind our own beeswax and be generous, because everyone has feelings, so please try!"

I'm not really sure what I'm saying now, but it feels good to let it all gush out.

"Wow." Caleb comes over when I'm finally out of words. "That was awesome."

"What was?"

"You," says Caleb. "The way you just calmed everybody down."

Did I really? This might be the first time that I have ever calmed anybody down.

And then my life gets even more unbelievable, because Victoria steps up to me.

"I'm really sorry," she says.

"I believe you," I say back.

Twenty-six

Hopper

Quinny is so busy making a big speech that she doesn't notice me walking away.

I'm not in the mood for any more words. I walk to the yard guard. If you say you don't feel good, he'll let you go inside to see the nurse.

"Hopper, wait!" Quinny and Victoria catch up to me.

"Thanks for telling the truth, Hopper," says Victoria.

"You did a good thing," says Quinny.

I shrug. But my heart feels a little thrilled. "So did you," I tell her.

I think of the card I started making Quinny yesterday. I want to go home and finish it. She's so talented at people, friends, life. I don't know how to say it. But I know how to draw it.

"Hopper, want to play with us after school?" Quinny asks. "It's early dismissal."

I shake my head. "I have some stuff to do."

"You sure? Victoria and I might go skating," says Quinny. "Wanna come?"

Victoria looks surprised. "I didn't think you'd want to skate again after your big crash."

"Are you kidding? I love skating! My arm is all better and I can't wait to see Coach Zadie again and learn a pizza stop and show that ice who's boss."

Victoria and Quinny do this squealing-hopping thing that turns into a hug. I feel a pinch in my chest at how easy and comfortable their hug looks. It's never like that for me. Then they start talking about other stuff that makes no sense to me—swizzles? foot-stink spray?—so I wander away.

I don't feel left out. Just wiped out. I painted the Books & Buddies Bench, and talked to Victoria, and told the truth about Kaitlin. And now I'm done. I wish Thanksgiving break would start right now and I could just go home and stay in my room the whole time.

If I were a car, my gas tank would say EMPTY.

The last thing I'm in the mood for is chorus, but that's what I have to do before I can go home. I slouch in the back row and mumble through "Jingle Bells." Quinny's up front, bellowing the words and banging her wood block. Ms. Bing keeps waving her hands at us, like a real conductor. I should be looking at her, but I can't help staring at Quinny up there, swaying and bopping, making nutty faces, having the time of her life.

I don't know how she does it.

On my way out of chorus I hear Alex snickering and joking to Xander and Johnnie. I hear him say "Quinny Dumble" again.

Even though Principal Ramsey talked to him, and to all of us, about bullying. Even though he knows it's wrong to call people names.

My hands ball up into fists. I'm so tired. And people are so awful.

I can't take it anymore. I can't accept it.

I go up to Alex by the lockers a moment later.

"If I ever hear you call Quinny that name again, I'll tell everyone how you peed your pants at my house."

It was all the way back in kindergarten, when our parents still made us play together.

Mom had to loan him a pair of my jeans.

Alex just stares at me, like I'm joking. I stare right back at him, like I'm not joking.

He's bigger than me. He's meaner than me. I can feel my heart pounding in my ears.

"I mean it," I tell him.

At dismissal, Quinny leaves with Victoria.

The bus ride home is much calmer without her sitting next to me. Calmer but lonelier.

When we get to my stop, I don't have energy for the chickens, so I go straight home. Mom asks if I'm okay. Then she asks what's wrong. Then she asks if I want to go for a run. She says a run will make me feel better. But all I want is to go upstairs to my room.

My room feels like a gas station, and I go there to fill my tank with things like reading, and drawing, and juggling, and taking care of my aquarium, and putting together human anatomy models, which are like 3-D puzzles of body parts. I've already put together models of an eye, a heart, and a foot. They're incredible, even if I'm the only one in my class who thinks so.

I take out my newest model: an ear. But it's not just some Mr. Potato Head ear you snap on a cartoon head—this thing is complicated. The human ear is divided into three main parts—outer ear, middle ear, and inner ear—and each part is filled with even more (and tinier) parts. Things like tubes and canals and spirals and ducts and drums—some of which are smaller than a pencil tip. The stapes bone in your middle ear is actually the tiniest bone in the human body.

Luckily my ear model is three times the size of a real human ear, so I can see what I'm doing. As I attach the malleus to the incus, deep inside by the eardrum, I hear my brothers downstairs, hollering and banging into furniture. I'm not sure why they're home—normally they go straight from school to soccer. I wish this ear model came with earplugs.

I'm connecting a semicircular duct to the cochlea when someone knocks at my door.

From the knock, I can tell who it is.

I open the door and Piper stares up at me, all somber. She comes over sometimes, asking to play chess. She doesn't usually say much, which is fine with me. I don't say much, either, which seems to be fine with her.

"Did you read to the chickens yet?" she says.

"Creeeeeepy," wails Ty, in my doorway now, too, looking inside.

I guess he noticed all the ear bones on my desk.

"Watch out, he dug those up at a cemetery." Trevor's behind him, trying to scare Piper.

But my brothers have it all wrong. I don't like anatomy models because they're creepy. I like them because I'm curious about people, and this is what people are like on the inside. I don't see what's so creepy about that.

"You are one weird little dude," says Ty.

"The weird bone's connected to the dork bone,"

sings Trevor. "The dork bone's connected to the fart bone—"

"Trevor," says Mom, behind them. "Come on, boys, your ride's here."

"The fart bone's connected to the—"

"Do *not* go there, Trevor," says Mom. "Not unless you want a repeat of last week."

Last week, Trevor got grounded for writing something inappropriate on the car window. He breathed on it to make it foggy and then wrote backward so people outside could read it. I was impressed he could write backward, but he didn't get any bonus points for that with Mom.

Instead of finishing his smelly song, Trevor hugs me from behind, so hard that my legs swing up, and then he gives me a noogie. I'm starting to get that he does this to people he likes. Both of my brothers do. Luckily, they don't bug me as much as they used to, since I had my tonsils out last month and my parents said they had to be gentler with me or lose their video games.

"Guess what?" Piper whispers, after the twins leave for soccer.

"What?"

"I think the chickens are really bored," she says.

Without asking permission, she goes and picks out a book from my shelves.

It's *Harold and the Purple Crayon.* One of my favorites from when I was little.

Even before I ever read it, I already did what Harold in the book does. I took myself places by drawing them. I learned about people and things by drawing them. It almost felt like Harold in the book was copying me. (But I know he wasn't, since his story was written in 1955.)

"Ms. Rivers, my teacher last year, used to say that books aren't things you have. They're places you go," I tell Piper. "I hope you get her for second grade, too."

Piper holds the book up, all hopeful. I love that she wants to go read to the chickens. But still, I don't want to be with anyone right now. Thanksgiving is going to be long and loud tomorrow, and I need some alone time. I want to finish my ear model, and work on my card for Quinny. I want to make Quinny smile when she sees it. I want to make her proud of herself.

"Some other time, Piper. Sorry, I just feel like being by myself."

"Me, too," she says.

She stands there, stubborn and small, waiting for me to get moving.

And I realize that maybe Piper and I can be by ourselves, together. At least for a little while. We're pretty good at it when we play chess, after all.

So I get up and follow her, and Harold and his crayon, over to the cooped-up chickens.

Twenty-seven

Quinny

I would never brag about this at school, but my family does the *best* Thanksgiving. We always go to my cousins Gemma and Sal's apartment in New York City and from their roof we can see all the Macy's parade balloons float by. Aunt Carla is actually in that parade—she's a balloon pilot in charge of a whole balloon (a different one every year), and she walks backward for the entire parade wearing a white jumpsuit and a green pilot cap and headset. She also wears a necklace with instructions for what to do with the balloon if it gets really windy or stormy. She's never been on TV, but she has a very, very, extra-very important job.

After the parade, Aunt Carla always lets me

try on that green pilot cap, and I pretend I'm in charge of one of those magnificent balloons! And Uncle Rex cooks a turkey in his Big Green Egg (which is like an outside grill but in the shape of an egg) and it's all smoky and savory, like a barbecue turkey. The turkey skin is so crackly-juicy-sweet that you could just eat that for dinner, though I guess that'd be a little gross. And after dinner, there's always lots of pie. (Sweet-potato pie counts as a vegetable, though, so we eat it with dinner.)

After all the food there is always music. My cousin Sal is ten and plays the guitar, and my cousin Gemma is almost thirteen and sings, and they have a brand-new four-year-old sister named Lilia who they adopted last year and she's awesome at shaking a tambourine. I bring my accordion and we take requests and sing and play and talk, and we always stay up too late and feel exhausted the next day but it's worth it.

Maybe the grown-ups argue a little, too, but we don't pay them much attention.

All of this excitement happens back in New York City, where we used to live before moving to Whisper Valley, so this morning we have a long drive back there. Mom wakes us up early and we pack up the car with food and extra clothes and air mattresses, so we can sleep on my cousins' living room floor tonight because we don't want to drive home late with stuffed bellies. I can't wait for the parade, the turkey, the music, the sleepover with my cousins, and all the noise and excitement that I miss so much. I can't wait to get on the road!

But just as we are pulling out of the driveway, Mom gets a call from Uncle Rex.

"Uh-huh. . . . Oh no. . . . Oh dear. . . . I'm so sorry, hang in there. . . . No, no, don't worry about us."

"Mom, what is it?"

Mom turns to us in the backseat with a frowny face. "Change of plans, guys. Aunt Carla and Sal woke up this morning with stomach bugs."

She says Thanksgiving at my cousins' apartment is canceled and we're staying home.

Oh no! I hope they feel better soon.

And I don't even know what we're going to eat since we didn't get a turkey to cook.

"Okay, Plan B," says Dad. "Vegetable lasagna from the freezer. Or maybe Mrs. Porridge can spare a chicken?"

"Daddy, bite your tongue! Mrs. Porridge loves those chickens—"

"She does not."

"You can't just eat someone's pet chicken. And she isn't home anyway."

Victoria told me that she, her dad, and aunt Myrna, who is also called Mrs. Porridge, are spending Thanksgiving at a senior citizen home, serving meals and talking with the seniors. Mom calls Mrs. Porridge to see if we could also volunteer there today, but they already have more volunteers than they need.

I know Hopper won't be home, either. He's going to watch his mom run some race, and then go to his aunt LuAnne's house. "Let's go eat at Cracker Barrel," I say. "I saw on a billboard they have yummy turkey dinner platters."

"I'd rather not spend Thanksgiving at a restaurant," says Daddy. "We'll be fine at home. Nothing wrong with staying put and being grateful for what we already have."

"I agree," says Mom. "I just hope Aunt Carla and Sal feel better soon."

Piper doesn't want to stay home, so she starts

crying, and then Cleo starts crying, and Daddy turns around and sticks a Binky in her face. Mom starts arguing with Daddy about *why-are-you-still-giving-her-that-Binky* and Daddy argues back and it doesn't exactly look like we are giving thanks for anything.

"Everyone, stop, stop! Okay, so Mom and Daddy want to stay home, but Piper and I want to go somewhere. I've got an idea that's called a compromise."

Daddy laughs. "Listen to you."

"Yes, listen to me. A compromise"—I turn to Piper—"is when we get some of what we want, and they get some of what they want. Now, what food do we have in the car, exactly?"

"Pie," says Mom. "Three pies. Pecan, apple, and pumpkin, exactly."

"Okay, great. That's what I was hoping you'd say."

"Quinny, what are you up to?" says Daddy.

I'm definitely up to something. I tell my idea for a compromise slow and calm, with words full of manners.

And Daddy looks at me like I just landed here from Mars, but in a good way.

Twenty-eight

Hopper

Aunt LuAnne is having Thanksgiving at her house. That means we all have to go to it.

But first we get to go cheer Mom on as she runs the Turkey Trot 5K race.

I don't cheer as loud as my brothers, but I cheer louder than I ever have before. Mom worked so hard training for this. I watch her and push her along with my eyes. *Go-go-go.*

She's in the back of the pack of runners.

But toward the end of the race, she speeds up. And my heart goes *go-go-go* all over again. I like the look on Mom's face. She's tired, but she's not giving up.

I watch her cross that finish line, with her

hands up and her smile glowing, and I run over and give her a hug. Mom is the easiest person in the world for me to hug. Even though right now she's sweaty. She didn't come in first, or even twenty-first, but she grabs me tight and laughs.

As soon as I'm ages twelve and up, I'm going to run this race with her.

I'm going to pace myself. I'm going to finish strong.

Later, after the race, we go to Aunt LuAnne's house, and it's the same.

Same people, same food, same thing as last year.

Aunt LuAnne's house is bigger than ours, and filled with my cousins Max and Ally, who are little, and a bunch of rough teenage cousins who my brothers like to hang out with.

There's no one here my size or my style, and I'm used to that.

But this year, when it's time to sit down for dinner, there's one big change.

My cousin Max is old enough to move from his high chair to a regular chair at the kids' table.

That bumps me off the kids' table and up to the big dining room table.

Actually, it bumps me up to a folding table that Aunt LuAnne puts next to the real dining room table and covers with a white tablecloth, to pretend that it's all one table.

I knock my knee against the diagonal metal bar that runs under the folding table.

Ouch! I actually remember this metal bar—I knocked my head on it at Aunt LuAnne's July Fourth BBQ party last summer. That was such a hot, crowded day. I just wanted to get out of the heat, and away from all the noise. So I crawled under this table and sat there, eating my lunch.

"Hopper? What about you?" says Aunt LuAnne.

Everyone is staring at me now. Every year Aunt LuAnne goes around the room and makes us say what we're grateful for. Every year I get nervous and mumble something, but all the good things to say are usually taken by the time it's my turn. And I guess I've been zoning out—thinking about that hot, crowded July Fourth party, and how I hid under the table—so I missed hearing the answers that other people just gave.

What if I say I'm grateful for the exact same thing as the person before me?

"Hopper, is there anything you're especially grateful for this year?" Aunt LuAnne repeats herself, gently. Dad looks at me, less gently. He's waiting to hear my answer.

But then the doorbell rings. And my answer walks right in.

It's Quinny Bumble, along with her family.

Which makes no sense. And yet it makes perfect sense.

Because she's what I'm grateful for. She changed my year. She changed my life.

"Hopper Hopper Hopper! We brought pie! Everyone in New York was barfing, so we couldn't go there, so we ate a boring vegetable lasagna at home and then your spectacular aunt let us invite ourselves here for dessert, wasn't that nice of her? Thank you, Aunt LuAnne! We brought pie! Which is your favorite: pecan, pumpkin, or apple? I love pecan the best!"

Quinny slips right into talking with everybody, just like that, and soon we're back to the gratitude speeches and it's her turn.

"I'm grateful for pie, and for Aunt LuAnne letting us come over, and for my family, and my friends, especially that one—" She points to me. "And oh oh! I'm grateful for the new and improved *save the cookies!* petition, and all the new chickens that Hopper and I are taking care of, and also for my guinea pig Crescent, who I named after my favorite dinner rolls that I make myself, except Mom just has to turn on the oven for me, and I'm grateful for the skating rink and swimming pool and rec soccer and—"

"What?" says Trevor. "What do you mean *rec* soccer?"

"I mean, I'm going to switch to rec soccer from now on, because it's once a week instead of a bunch of times, so I'll still have time for cannonballs and public sessions and—"

"Are you nuts?" says Trevor.

"You'll never make the club team if you do rec soccer," says Ty.

"Then I guess I'll just play soccer at recess."

"*What?*" the twins say—they almost spit—at the same time.

Quinny's parents don't seem to care if she

does rec soccer, or recess soccer, but my own dad chuckles and shakes his head. "Quinny, you have a gift," he says.

"I do? Where is it?" She looks around the room.

Dad smiles, like this is a joke. "I'm serious, Quinny, it's worth developing," he says. "You've got great timing, great instincts, you're aggressive and agile and—"

"Thank you, Mr. Grey, but I've already done a ton of fancy soccer this fall, and now the rest of my life wants a turn at some fun, too. I want to improve my cannonball, and I need to feed the new chickens more or they'll never get to know me. And, by the way, Mom, I want to go back to skating class with Victoria, too."

"You want to go back to the place you almost broke your arm?" asks Mrs. Bumble.

"Of course!"

People are talking in smaller groups now, but Aunt LuAnne takes control of all the talking again and keeps asking for more gratitude answers, and then it's back to me.

"Hopper?" she says. "Your turn. What are you grateful for this year?"

There is a big silence now. So big that nothing I say could ever fill it.

I wish I were a poet, or a comedian, or even just interesting.

But all I can be is myself.

"I'm grateful to be sitting here with everyone at this table," I finally say.

Instead of hiding under it by myself, I don't say.

Twenty-nine

Quinny

The problem with cleaning my room is that Mom always picks the nicest, sunniest days to make me do it. Like now, on this last afternoon of Thanksgiving break, while my sisters are outside with Hopper and the chickens, I'm stuck in here trying to organize my desk, because Mom decided we're going to start taking homework seriously and get on a schedule and do it IN THE SAME PLACE EVERY SINGLE TIME. But honestly, I don't think sitting at my desk is going to make me understand decimals any better.

Mom sometimes gets in this mood where she wants life to be perfect—but luckily the mood never lasts very long, and everything eventually goes back to normal.

Finally, after lots of pain and suffering, my desk is clean-ish and Mom says *good enough* and I'm free! I run over to the Chalet des Poulets, where Hopper and Piper are reading a story out loud, and Walter is lounging in the sun, and all the chickens are out hopping around and *brrruuping* and *bipping* and *bockbockbocking*. Poodle flaps up to peck at a cabbage piñata hanging on a rope. Pumpkin rolls a broken mushy pumpkin and makes a happy mess. Polar Bear kicks a nubby ball around with my baby sister Cleo.

"Mrs. Porridge, look! Did you notice these chickens aren't trying to kill each other anymore, and they don't look scared or confused?"

"I noticed," says Mrs. Porridge, sitting on her porch. "Turns out the chickens love a good story. Calms them down. We also brought out a few odds and ends, to give them some exercise and keep them out of trouble. They've sorted themselves out, and figured out who's in charge."

"They have? Who?"

"Look around, Quinny."

I do. And what I notice is a big surprise, actually.

I would have guessed Walter would become a bossy rooster-cat in charge, or Pumpkin, whose beak is a fierce weapon, or even Polar Bear, because she's ten times the size of a regular chicken. But it's Cha-Cha who gets my attention.

Cha-Cha shrieks when Pumpkin won't share her sticky pumpkin with Poodle. Cha-Cha nudges Polar Bear to keep playing when she tries to go back in the henhouse. Cha-Cha *bips* and *bocks* up at Poodle when she flaps too high up in the rafters.

And then Cha-Cha hops onto Walter, like a tiny queen on her furry throne. She stares out at the Chalet des Poulets like it's hers to rule, and clucks out a speech.

I was wrong this whole time—Cha-Cha isn't Walter's sidekick. He's hers.

"But Mrs. Porridge, how can Cha-Cha be in charge? She's the smallest and youngest."

"You don't have to be loud or large to be a leader, Quinny," says Mrs. Porridge. "You just

have to be observant, hardworking, and care a lot about your fellow chickens."

"Well, I think Cha-Cha is doing a great job. These chickens look so happy."

And then I notice that Piper looks happy, too. Even though I know this reading-out-loud stuff isn't easy for her. She can't say every word in the story, but she's trying. If she doesn't know a word, she doesn't just skip over it, she stays there and doesn't give up and Hopper helps her try it again, over and over, until she kind-of-sort-of says it right.

When you try stuff over and over, that's called practicing. I remember Hopper told me he practiced diving a lot before he figured out how to do a good dive.

Another thing I notice is that Piper is really, truly, absolutely improving. With each new page, she gets more of the words right.

I guess it's not shocking. If you work hard at something, you might get better at it.

My pizza stop might get better if I practice it. My cannonball, too, I bet.

My math might even get better, just maybe.

Piper and Hopper sitting there together remind me a little of me and Ms. Jasani.

Slow down. Take it one step at a time. Keep trying. Stay positive. Don't give up.

If Piper can learn to say a whole book out loud, and those chickens can learn to get along, then I can probably-definitely learn some measly decimals.

* * *

So on Monday I go back to Math Lounge and listen to every word Ms. Jasani says, even the ones I don't understand. (Usually I stop paying attention when I don't understand something, but this time I try harder to stop my brain from running away.)

We do another cookie word problem, and this time I finish it before the bell rings. Ms. Jasani gives me another real cookie, which I chomp right there so we don't get caught breaking Principal Ramsey's mean food rules.

I go over math again on the bus home with Hopper. And he asks me to explain it to *him*, like I am the teacher and he is a kid, and, surprise, that turns out to be really helpful.

At night, I go over my math again with Daddy, because he is less tired and crabby than Mom for a change.

And a funny thing happens. The more I go over my decimals, the closer I feel to actually almost understanding them. Not all the way. I still lose track of those decimal dots, but I find them again more quickly. I don't worry as much, and my breathing feels slower.

By the end of my day, I still don't like math very much.

But I like that I feel less nervous about it.

In bed that night, I can't stop wiggling.

My least favorite kind of Monday is the kind after a long holiday weekend, when you kind of forgot about school, but then school pokes you on the shoulder and goes *hey, I'm still here and I OWN you, hahahahaha.* But this wasn't that kind of Monday, it really wasn't!

I took my whole day one step at a time.

One decimal dot at a time.

One autograph at a time. (I got a lot of new people to sign my new and improved petition at recess, and I even turned it in to Principal Ramsey!)

One bang on the wood block at a time. (We had a double practice in chorus today, since the Winter Holiday Assembly is coming up soon.)

One breath and one hello and one raised hand at a time.

I also made a big decision today: I'm getting rid of the word *dummy* from all my sentences.

It's a dumb word. (Oops! I meant bad.) It hurts people's feelings. It hurts my own feelings when I say it. I don't think anybody deserves to be called that word, not even me.

I'm no dummy. I'm just a kid, trying my best.

On Tuesday I wake up ready for another great day, but when I get to school something sour happens that destroys all my hope.

Ms. Jasani is absent from Math Lounge. So I have to stay in my class for math.

And Mrs. Flavio passes out a math quiz.

I shoot my hand up. "Mrs. Flavio, I really, really have to use the bath—"

"Relax, Quinny, I'll get to you in a second." She gives me a *pipe-down* look.

Then, a bunch of seconds later, she tells me that I don't have to take this quiz. I can sit in the back and work on my own worksheets from Ms. Jasani.

Phew! This means I won't have to go hide in the bathroom now.

But, wait a minute.

I realize I actually *do* want to take that quiz.

Because maybe I'm a math expert now from all my hard work yesterday. I know how to do things one step at a time now. I can just do that quiz one problem at a time, no problem.

I explain this to Mrs. Flavio and she gives me a tired look and says, "Okay, Quinny, if that's what you want. No harm in giving it a try."

She gives me my very own copy of that quiz, and I sit down and look at it.

I look a little harder. There are twelve questions on this quiz. That's three or four too many, if you ask me. I wait for the first question to make sense in my head.

It should happen any second now.

I fidget in my seat. Math is much easier when you're sitting on a big bouncy ball, like the kind Ms. Jasani has, instead of this hard classroom chair. I feel like whistling, but that's not allowed during quizzes. I try my best to look like a genuine, brilliant quiz taker. But this quiz is much harder than my math with Ms. Jasani. I understand some of the questions. And *some* of *some* of the other questions. But mostly I just take my best guesses.

When the time is up, there are two questions left that I didn't even get to.

Everyone is passing up their quizzes. I have no choice but to turn mine in, too.

I bet I flunked that quiz. I probably got the lowest score in my whole class.

I shoot my wiggly hand straight up in the air.

I am not going to cry. Not until I get to the bathroom, at least.

I guess I can't stay in this bathroom forever.

I splash cold water on my face one last time. I look at my drippy chin in the mirror.

Back by the lockers, Hopper comes up to me and says, "Quinny, are you okay?"

"Absolutely. Sure. Except I flunked that math quiz and I just want to go home."

"You don't know that you flunked."

"You don't know that I *didn't*."

"Quinny, I have something for you."

Hopper hands me a card he's been holding behind his back. The cover looks serious and official. Except there's also an orange-polka-dotted chicken on it.

"Hopper, what is this thing?" I open it up. I flip through the pages.

PROGRESS REPORT: Whisper Valley Elementary School

Student name: Eleanor Quinston Bumble
Nickname: Quinny
Grade: 3

1. Schoolbus Studies
SCHOOL BUS
A+

2. Hallway Arts
A+

3. Lunch-ematics
SALAD
Bread
Egg
A+

4. Recess-ology
A+

5. Friendship muscles
A+

6. Sharing Skills
A+

And I can't believe my eyes. Because this isn't just a card . . . it's a report card.

Thirty

Hopper

Quinny flips through the card I just gave her. She looks confused.

Then she smiles. And giggles.

Seeing her gloomy face get brighter because of something I did feels pretty great.

"Hopper, this is the silliest thing I've ever seen."

I know how to be silly. I just don't blast it out for the whole world to notice.

I love making Quinny laugh, but the pictures I drew in her report card–card are no joke. Everything in there is the truth, from stuff I really saw her do.

Quinny turns to the last page of it. She gasps.

A real person's eyes cannot boing out of their head like a cartoon person's. That's impossible. But Quinny's eyes come close. And then she flings her arms out and wraps them around my shoulders. I'm like a prisoner now. It's hard to breathe.

I've been hugged by Quinny before. I'm not

going to panic. It'll be over soon. But this hug goes on longer than the others. I raise my arms to push her away, but they don't actually do that. They wrap around Quinny and squeeze her back, for the first time ever.

A both-ways Quinny hug feels much different from a one-way Quinny hug.

It feels much better. That's all I can really say about it.

Thirty-one

Quinny

You're not supposed to hug another person without their permission. I know that.

But sometimes I forget stuff I already know.

Hopper wiggles inside my strong, happy hug.

I'm just so excited, because I've never been on the honor roll before—never, ever! Wait until my parents find out. And Mrs. Flavio and Ms. Jasani and Principal Ramsey and Mrs. Porridge and Piper and everyone!

I've also never been hugged back by Hopper's very own arms before.

I don't know which is more exciting. It could be a tie.

Hopper wiggles some more. I loosen my grip on him. But I don't ever want to let go of this moment where he showed me all the incredible, brilliant A-pluses I got just for being me.

"Hopper, did you know I'm going to put this in a frame?" I whisper into his ear. "Thank you for being my best friend in the whole round world."

Thirty-two

Hopper

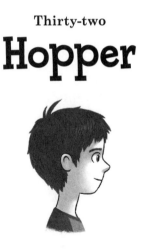

Mom forgot to close my window shade last night, so I wake up early on Wednesday from all the morning light. I don't mind. The house is quiet now. I get up and find some scrap paper.

A Little Free Library isn't free. Everything in life costs money. I write down how much I have:

$10 from giving Quinny swimming lessons for the past two Saturdays.

$8 from cleaning out the chicken coop last week. (I convinced Mrs. Porridge to pay me in money, not eggs.)

$1.04 in coins I found in the sofa cushions. (Dad said finders keepers.)

$1.53 in coins I found on the floor and seat pockets of the car. (Mom said the same.)

$5 from Aunt Cindy in St. Charles, Illinois, who sent it in my birthday card last month.

$11.39 from a birthday gift from Victoria, which I returned, because I'm not into paint-your-own birdhouses. Mom said it was okay to return it, but that I didn't need to tell Victoria.

$35 from the money Mom promised me from her Turkey Trot 5K race sponsors.

All of that adds up to $71.96.

A woman I spoke to on the phone at a lumberyard told me it will cost $90 to buy enough wood to make the Little Free Library. That means we only need $18.04 more.

I can't wait to tell Quinny that we're getting closer.

In the kitchen, my brothers stick French-toast sticks up their noses instead of dunking them in syrup. Mom hands me a breakfast plate, too, but I've kind of lost my appetite.

"Hon, Grandpa Gooley called," she says. "He got ahold of some extra lumber, after all."

"Really? How much?"

"Not enough to build the whole thing, I don't think, but a good amount," she says. "You can call him back after school. Boys, time to get moving," Mom reminds my brothers. "Please remove all food from your nostrils and go find your backpacks."

My brothers carpool to middle school with a bunch of big kids, and that's fine with me.

On the way to the bus stop, I hear crying coming from Quinny's house. That's not unusual.

Her family bursts outside and trails behind me. Cleo is wailing, Piper is whining, and Quinny is arguing. Their dad roars, "Quinny, please!" and "Piper, that's enough!" He digs around in his pocket and finds a Binky and sticks it in Cleo's mouth. Right away Cleo quiets down.

That's one out of three.

"Oooh, Mom said you're not supposed to give her Binkies anymore," says Quinny.

"Mom's not the one whose eardrums are about to explode," says Quinny's dad. "Good morning, Hopper. I hope you've had a calmer morning than we have."

If you don't count my brothers sticking break-fast up their noses, I have.

When the school bus pulls up to our stop, Mr. Bumble groans—he just noticed that Piper is only wearing one shoe. He rushes back home with Cleo and Piper while Quinny and I get on the bus. I tell her that the Little Free Library lumber costs $90, and I already have $71.96, so we need just $18.04 more. But we might not need it at all, because of Grandpa Gooley's free wood.

"Hey, that's kind of like Ms. Jasani's word problems, except with wood instead of cookies," she says.

"Cookies?" says Xander, sitting behind us. "What cookies? You've got cookies?"

"Nope, no cookies," says Quinny. "Nothing to see here."

Then she smiles and shushes me. I'm the only one Quinny told about the cookies in Math Lounge. She doesn't want to get Ms. Jasani in trouble. We aren't allowed to have cookies in classrooms any-more, but I think those cookies might actually be helping Quinny. I've been doing math with her on the bus all week, and she's definitely getting less scared of decimals.

After morning meeting, Principal Ramsey's voice makes some announcements over the loudspeaker. The last one is that there will be a special delivery today, because Victoria Porridge just donated a Little Free Library to our school.

"Thanks to Victoria Porridge and her family for this generous donation," he says. "It will provide a sheltered space for books on the playground, and make the Books & Buddies Bench area an even more exciting place to spend recess."

Everyone in class looks over at Victoria. Quinny starts clapping, and everyone joins in. My chest hurts. My breath feels stuck in my throat.

I'm the only one not clapping, so I force myself to.

Quinny looks over at me. "Wow! Isn't that exciting, Hopper? Now you don't have to worry about making a Little Free Library at all!"

Victoria looks over at me, too. I wish she'd look at someone else. I don't know what her Little Free

Library will be like, or if it'll have room for all the books I was imagining. I try to forget about my own ideas, because her idea is the one that's coming true.

Kids start talking to Victoria. "I told Daddy about it," she says. "And he thought it was a great idea, so we just ordered one online. It should be here by recess. It can fit one hundred and twenty-five books and is made of solid teak, which is the best kind of wood."

Victoria's Little Free Library sounds impressive.

I'm sure it will be better than anything I could ever make.

Later that morning, Mrs. Flavio returns the math quizzes from yesterday. I got a 100.

Quinny looks at hers and bops up and down. "Wow! No way! I got a 75! Which Mrs. Flavio bumped up to a 78 because of extra credit, and that's almost a B!"

Victoria puts her arm around Quinny. "Congratulations, that's great news."

"I drew a little doodle to explain this one problem and got extra credit because it was made out of parts of a cookie, which are kind of like fractions, so that's how I got my almost-a-B. I can't believe it!"

"Well done, Quinny," says Mrs. Flavio.

"Oh, Mrs. Flavio, thank you. I couldn't have done it if you hadn't sent me to Ms. Jasani in Math Lounge! I need to go thank her, too, right this very minute."

I want to say congratulations to Quinny, too. I've been helping her with math on the bus, so I know how hard she's been working. But she runs out of the room without looking at me.

I touch my arm to make sure I'm still here.

Yup.

I look at it to make sure I'm not invisible.

Nope.

At lunch, there is another announcement over the loudspeaker in the cafeteria.

"Folks, we've got some more big news. . . ." It's Principal Ramsey's voice, again. "Our new food policy has changed, in response to a student petition. We still believe that too much sugar is not good for growing bodies, and we want to be more mindful of students with allergies. But we also believe in listening to feedback as we shape our school community. This petition was created by a persistent young lady, Quinny Bumble, and signed by many of you. We used it to reach a compromise. Going forward, we'll allow peanut- and tree-nut-free desserts at your class winter holiday parties. For birthdays, we'll be consolidating nut-free treats each month into *one* celebration per classroom. Hot lunch remains dessert-free, and the rule against eating in classrooms stands, except for the winter holiday party and monthly birthdays. For more details, see the flyer going home today. Thanks for your attention, and enjoy your lunch."

After Principal Ramsey finishes talking, everyone else starts talking. It sounds like a swarm of bees just invaded the cafeteria.

Wow. The petition worked. We'll get sweets at our winter holiday party next week. We'll still get birthday treats once a month. Principal Ramsey listened to us. He compromised.

I look over at Quinny, who is surrounded by kids.

"Quinny, you're awesome," says Xander.

"You rock," says Izzy.

"Thanks, Quinny," says Caleb.

"Nice job, Big Foot," says Alex.

Even Victoria, who didn't like the petition, says congratulations on getting Principal Ramsey to change the rules. "That's hard to do. It must have been a really smart petition."

I kind of get bumped out of the way as people try to get closer to Quinny.

No one says anything to me. No one's proud of me.

I head toward the restroom at the end of the cafeteria. It's calmer there.

By the door, I look back at her. The more people come at her, the more she glows and chats, bounces and laughs. The petition worked. Everyone is happy. Quinny is a superstar.

And I suddenly feel like I'm shrinking.

Thirty-three

Quinny

That petition did such a great job!

Everyone rushes up to me like I'm famous, except Hopper.

He's the one I really want to celebrate with, but he's been acting funny all day.

He barely said thanks to Victoria for the Little Free Library she got us. He didn't jump for joy about my amazing almost-a-B on the math quiz. (Not even a tiny little yay.) And when Principal Ramsey compromised and said yes to cookies for the holiday party, Hopper's face did nothing. Really, truly, absolutely nothing.

It's hard to tell what's going on inside his head, sometimes.

I thought he'd be happy about Victoria giving us a Little Free Library, since now he doesn't have to spend any money or make one himself.

I thought he'd be proud of my quiz, since he helps me with math so much on the bus.

I thought he'd be thrilled the new and improved petition changed Principal Ramsey's mind about cookies, since he's the one who new-and-improved it with his brainy compromise.

The bell rings for recess, and I look around for Hopper, but he's gone.

I guess I just don't understand that boy.

Thirty-four

Hopper

At recess, I watch from behind the slide as a man rolls a big crate across the playground.

"Mr. Delivery Man, wait!" Quinny chases after him. "Is that what I think it is?"

"Depends on what you think it is, kid."

He wheels the crate over to the Books & Buddies Bench.

A crowd comes around. A bunch of teachers and kids watch the man open the crate.

It's the Little Free Library that Victoria got us from her father.

It's carved from wood, and fancy, and huge.

Principal Ramsey stands in between the Little Free Library and the Books & Buddies

Bench, which I just finished painting yesterday. He talks and gestures to the bench, and then the Little Free Library, but I can't tell what he is saying. Victoria is right there by him, smiling out at everyone around them. She's wearing a complicated dress. The bottom part of the dress swishes as she walks around and hands out bookmarks. She almost twirls from person to person. I hide farther behind the slide so she can't see me.

Victoria is the center of attention.

I am not the center of attention, even though the Little Free Library was my idea, and so was the Books & Buddies Bench.

I feel like raising my hand to point this out. But we're on the playground, where people don't really raise their hands. And I don't want to go anywhere near Victoria.

"Hopper."

The voice saying my name makes me jump a little. It's Juniper, behind me, staring.

I stare back at her.

"Why are you hiding?" she asks.

"Why don't you ever sing in chorus?" I ask.

She's been pretending to sing all year. Sometimes I'm tempted to tell Ms. Bing.

Juniper doesn't answer my question, and I don't answer hers.

But she stays with me, under the slide, for the rest of recess, and that feels okay.

At dismissal, Victoria comes up to me by the lockers.

"Hopper, you didn't take a bookmark at recess."

It's almost time to get in the bussers line. I'm really not in the mood for this.

"I have some extras." She holds out a bookmark.

When I don't take it, her hand shakes a little.

Fine. I take the bookmark. I put it in my backpack without looking at it.

"So, what do you think of the Little Free Library?" she asks.

I shrug. I didn't like all the hoopla at recess. It didn't have much to do with reading. It was more about Victoria, so I stayed away.

"It's fine."

I can tell Victoria wants me to say more. But I'm not in the mood to tell her how great she is.

Besides, it's almost December. Soon it'll be too cold to sit outside and read at recess, anyway. Then I won't have to think about Victoria's Little Free Library until spring.

It was a stupid idea in the first place.

Thirty-five

Quinny

In the bussers line, I try to talk to Hopper. But he says he forgot something in his locker and runs back to get it, and then he goes to the end of the line instead of coming back to me.

And hey, I think that is called blowing me off.

On the bus, he sits next to Darla, the bus aide, up front, instead of walking back to our seat.

I just had the best day ever, but Hopper looks like he had the worst. And I don't really know why, so I get up and walk to the front of the bus to see what's going on.

Darla says, "Keep your distance, Quinny, he could hurl at any moment."

Oh, that's not good. I didn't know Hopper was sick. He won't even look at me.

"Piper has extra saltines in her backpack," I tell him, but he doesn't answer.

I go back to my seat, by myself. *By myself* is never my favorite way to do anything.

To cheer Hopper up, I talk to the kids around me about what a great day it's been, in my biggest voice, so that he can hear, too. I talk about the fancy Little Free Library we got at recess. And the almost-a-B I got on my math quiz. And the fabulous petition that changed Principal Ramsey's mind about cookies. And how I'll get to bake coconut snowballs for the holiday party.

But Hopper doesn't turn around or look cheered up by my words. He leans against the bus window and slumps there the whole ride home. By the time we get to our stop, his shaggy head is slumped practically sideways and I can see all of his soggy-foggy breath on that window.

Thirty-six

Hopper

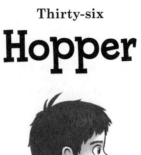

The truth is, I don't really feel like throwing up. But letting Darla think so means I get to sit up front. And, it makes people keep their distance.

But I can still hear Quinny talking from our usual seat farther back—talking and talking about why today was so great. I wish I agreed with her.

I know I don't make any sense to Quinny. I don't even make sense to myself, sometimes. My head is a jumble of sore, confusing thoughts. I want to run the Turkey Trot race, even though it's already over and I wasn't old enough. I want to raise money to build a Little Free Library, because it was my idea (not Victoria's). I want people to know I worked hard on the sweets petition to save our holiday party.

I don't want to be a superstar like Quinny. I don't want tons of attention.

I just wish I mattered a little.

There's no way I'm saying any of that out loud, of course.

I'm not the kind of person that people notice. And that's fine with me, usually.

But today, it stings.

When the bus pulls up at our stop, I get off first, before Quinny, before Piper even, because I was sitting way up front.

"Mom, can we go for a run?" I say, the second I see her.

I drag Mom away and she stumbles to keep up. "Hopper, wait . . . hold your horses."

"Mrs. Grey, why do people always say that?" Quinny follows us. "It's impossible to hold a horse! A chicken, maybe. And Hopper, didn't you have a stomachache on the bus?"

"What?" says Mom, all confused now.

I want to run away from Quinny's curiosity. I

want to put on my sneakers and go pound out all my confusion. I pull Mom away from Quinny. "I'm feeling better. Let's go for a run."

"But honey, Grandpa Gooley stopped by with the lumber for your library project."

"He can take it back. Victoria already did it, so nobody needs me anymore."

"What?"

"I said, I don't want the wood. Because Victoria took the Little Free Library idea and did it all by herself. She had her dad buy one."

"Oh, wow, that was generous of them—"

"So nobody needs me."

"Sweetie, I wouldn't put it that way," Mom says. "Slow down. What's going on?"

"Nothing."

It's too complicated to explain, and I don't want to try with Quinny nearby. She's still following me home, even though I didn't invite her.

"Bye," I say to her, as loudly as I can.

"Hopper, don't you want to play?" Quinny asks. "And feed the chickens?"

"You don't need me to feed the chickens."

"What?"

"You don't need me for anything. Congratulations on your quiz, and your petition."

"Hopper, wait—"

But I don't.

Thirty-seven

Quinny

I see a lump bump up in Hopper's throat before he turns away and leaves. I see his shiny eyes. Of course I need him. Why would he say that? Why would he even think that?

I need his kind, quiet heart every day.

He's one of the biggest reasons my life is good.

But would he say the same about me? I don't know.

I go home and show Daddy my spectacular almost-a-B and tell him about Principal Ramsey's compromise on the petition. We bake a special snack to celebrate—hot, flaky crescent rolls filled with strawberry jam. But they don't taste as great without Hopper here.

Then Daddy reminds me that I forgot to feed the real live Crescent this morning, so I go over to his cage. Crescent loves munching timothy hay. He loves nibbling baby carrots. But Piper and Cleo are bothering us, and I can tell Crescent wants some privacy, so I take him upstairs in his little pouch. We go to my room and I shut the door. I cuddle him while he chews, and fill him in on life, and ask for some advice about Hopper.

Crescent doesn't answer, but he's an extremely good listener. I can tell he's thinking about it. Then I show him my wonderful, special, funny, very, very, extra-very unique report card–card that Hopper made just for me. I flip through it and show off every page.

Crescent spends a really long time sniffing my A-plus grades in *Friendship Muscles* and *One-of-a-Kindness*.

I think I have some studying to do.

Thirty-eight

Hopper

After trying and trying to make me talk about my feelings—no, thank you—Mom finally lets me go up to my room.

It's so much easier to just be by myself.

I read three chapters of *Astrophysics for People in a Hurry*, even though I am not in a rush.

I finish my ear model, carefully. There are so many moving parts; if just one part is out of whack, the whole thing won't click into place.

I draw another sketch of the Little Free Library. My version, not Victoria's, and with even more detail. It will never come true, but it's nice to have a drawing of it, at least.

Piper knocks on my door. As usual, I can tell it's her.

When I open it, she shows me a picture book with a chicken on the cover.

"Bock bock bock," she says.

"I can't, Piper, not today."

"Bock bock BOCK bock bock," Piper insists.

"Piper, you're not a chicken, you're a kid."

She *baaa baaaas* like a baby goat.

"Not that kind of kid. The human kind."

"Bock," says Piper, in a sad voice, and then switches to English. "The chickens need another story. I'll say it. You just come listen."

"What do you mean?" Piper doesn't know how to read yet.

"I learned the book. For the chickens."

"Are you serious? You can read this book?"

Piper nods. This I have to see. I walk with her over to the Chalet des Poulets.

And there is a lot going on here today.

Pumpkin is pecking at a bale of hay.

Poodle is climbing monkey bars made of branches and twigs.

Cha-Cha and Polar Bear are chatting while Walter rolls around licking his fur.

But when they spot us, they all stop what they are doing and gather around.

Quinny's here, too. She's hiding behind a bush, but not very well. She watches us.

"I can see you," I say to Quinny.

She walks over, slowly. It's strange to see Quinny do anything slowly.

"Is it okay if I'm here, too?" she asks.

"It's a free country," I answer.

She holds out some crumpled tinfoil. "Daddy and I made jammy crescent rolls. They're still hot."

I say no thanks. Even though they smell delicious.

Quinny sits down, but not too close. I appreciate that.

"Hopper, I'm sorry," she says.

"You have nothing to be sorry for," I say.

"Thank you for helping me with my math on the bus," she says. "And thank you for making the petition so new and improved. And thank you for living next door to me. And—"

"Quinny—"

"Wait, I'm not done yet. And thank you for thinking of the Little Free Library idea, even though Victoria is the one who actually bought it with her daddy's money. And thank you for forgiving me when I forgot to say thank you at school for everything you—"

"It's okay."

"I thought I said thank you, but then I realized that maybe I didn't do it out loud—"

"Quinny, shhh—" I point.

Piper has opened her picture book. She clears her throat and starts reading out loud. It takes her a while, but she reads that whole book, every page. She finishes and shuts the book and looks at me, her chin high up in the air.

I'm amazed. So are the chickens.

"Piper, that was really good," I tell her.

Piper beams. She runs off to play.

"She just memorized it," says Quinny. "That's not the same as reading, is it?"

"I think it still counts."

Memorizing a book seems pretty impressive

to me. I'm proud of Piper. I'm proud of myself for helping her. It feels good to help someone. It makes me feel less invisible.

"Juniper never sings in chorus," I tell Quinny.

"What?"

From the look on Quinny's face I can tell she means *who?* I don't know why I'm telling her this, except it just popped into my head.

"Juniper Dunne, in chorus," I say. "She's in the back row with me. She pretends to sing, but she just mouths the words."

"Oh. And you mean she never gets in trouble?"

"Ms. Bing doesn't even notice."

Maybe that's why Juniper doesn't sing. Because it makes no difference. No one cares. The sadness of this hits me hard. I'm not sure why I care that she never sings, but I do.

"Look," says Piper, in front of us again. Her face is bright with joy. In her cupped hands is a speckled, blue-brown egg. "I found it in the nest."

"Hopper Hopper Hopper, can you believe it?" cries Quinny, almost knocking that egg out of Piper's hand. "Finally, an egg! But who did it? Who laid that beautiful egg?"

We look around at all the chickens, but none of them take credit.

Mrs. Porridge comes into the Chalet des Poulets now, holding a large mirror.

"Mrs. Porridge, the chickens are laying eggs!" says Quinny. "One of them just laid a spectacular egg!!!"

"Calm down," says Mrs. Porridge. "I found a

few eggs this morning, too. They're starting to settle in and feel at home."

"Well, it's perfect timing! I'm going to need five eggs to make coconut snowballs for our class holiday party," says Quinny, turning to the chickens. "So get to work, guys, okay?"

"Mrs. Porridge, why are you putting a mirror in a chicken coop?" I ask.

"It's another way to keep them busy, help keep peace in the flock," she says. "These happen to be the silliest chickens in town. I thought it'd be highly entertaining if they could see how silly they looked, like watching the chicken channel on TV."

"Wait, you mean there's a chicken channel on TV?" Quinny asks.

"No, Quinny, that was my attempt at a joke."

"Mrs. Porridge, that was an excellent joke and this mirror is fantastic! Now these chickens can do hairstyles. Especially Poodle, who really needs a trim. They can see if they have dried worm bits on their faces, or if they missed a spot during their dust bath. Also, they can work on their dancing!"

"Exactly, Quinny. Just think of the possibilities."

Poodle shakes her tail feathers and clucks in

the new chicken mirror. Pumpkin tries to peck at her reflection. Quinny watches her own silly self as she dances. She laughs. She loses her balance. She laughs even louder, and waves me over. "Hopper, get over here, let's dance!"

I shake my head and try to hide my smile. No way.

She belongs on a stage, but I'd much rather be sitting in the audience.

The next morning, I see Quinny rushing to the bus stop, covered in white powder. Her dad's trying to wipe it off her head as he pushes Cleo in the stroller and hollers back for Piper to hurry up. He looks really annoyed.

"But Daddy, how was I supposed to know that bag of flour had a tiny little invisible hole in it?"

"You weren't supposed to climb up to the top shelf and touch it in the first place."

"I just wanted to make sure we have enough flour to make coconut snowballs—"

"Well now we don't, since it's all over the kitchen floor. Good morning, Hopper."

I nod good morning. I back up a little, to make

room for the Bumbles and all their drama. Piper comes up and leans against my arm, just a little. She's carrying another book.

"Daddy, I'm sorry, I'll make it up to you. I'll fold *all* the laundry on the dining table—"

"Quinny—"

"Even Piper's underpants."

"Quinny, please." Then Mr. Bumble turns to me. "Hopper, before I forget, I've been meaning to thank you for helping Piper with her language arts. She's become a lot more interested in books since you guys started reading to the chickens. How can we ever repay you?"

Mr. Bumble looks at me like I am a superhero. I feel myself standing taller.

Being thanked is the best feeling in the world.

I ride the bus to school and spend the rest of the morning with that best feeling inside me, like a quiet, glowing secret. I don't say much in class or at lunch. I take a book out to recess and sit on the stairs.

But then Victoria comes over to me. "Hopper, I need your help."

Great. I just had a conversation with her yesterday, and now she wants another one?

"It's about the Little Free Library," she says. "No one's using it."

I noticed that. Even I'm not using it. I'd rather just forget about the Little Free Library, and the Books & Buddies Bench. They're all hers. I'd rather sit on the stairs with my book again.

"Hopper, no one will use the Little Free Library if you're so far away from it," says Victoria. "Come sit on the Books & Buddies Bench. You're my best advertising."

"What?" No one has ever called me *advertising* before. I don't know what she means.

"You're the biggest reader in our class," she says. "Everyone knows you're the book expert. Tell me what's missing. I mean, the books from Aunt Myrna are great, but what other books should we get? I can ask my dad to order more. He's in Hong Kong right now, but he can do it long distance, or Masha can."

It must be nice being Victoria and snapping your fingers to get anything you want from your dad who's in Hong Kong or Argentina or Iceland, or wherever he went this week.

"I'll think about it," I answer, even though I don't want to. I just want her to go away.

"Maybe books about soccer for some of those boys who don't read a whole ton?" she says. "And books about horses since a bunch of girls ride horses? And what else? What does Quinny like to read about? I could even take special requests, if someone wants something we don't have. I just want it to be fun. We could start a book club and talk about books, too."

Is Victoria serious? She looks serious.

"You'd be in the club, of course," she says. "I mean, anybody could join, it's not a club to leave people out. I wouldn't do that."

I look at Victoria. Yeah, right. This is the girl who made the Smart List talking.

"When it's nice out, the club can meet by the Books & Buddies Bench and Little Free Library," she says. "When it's yucky out, we can meet in the school library, or maybe one of the teachers will let us meet in a classroom. We can take turns picking books to talk about."

I'm not saying it to Victoria, but that is not the worst idea in the world. I wouldn't mind talking as much if I could talk about books. And maybe other people would use the Little Free Library and Books & Buddies Bench more if there were a club to go with it.

"Also, I can bake bookies for every time the club meets," she says.

"Bake what?"

"Bookies—they're cookies in the shape of a book."

"What about Principal Ramsey's food rules?"

"He made a compromise for Quinny's petition. I bet I can convince him for a book club, too. Besides, my bookies are vegan—they're so healthy they're practically vegetables. But don't tell anyone that," she says. "I mean, they're also delicious."

"I won't." I try not to smile. I don't want Victoria to think I like talking to her.

But she looks at me now, and it is actually kind of a nice look. A hopeful look. I have to admit, she's creative. She took my Little Free Library idea and made it better, bigger. I was holding on to it so tight, but now it feels good to relax my grip a little. To share the idea.

Suddenly I understand what Victoria is standing here waiting for.

"Thank you for getting us that Little Free Library," I say to her.

"Thank you for thinking of it in the first place," she says to me. Then she bops up and down, like Quinny, but not as fast. "So you'll join the book club?"

Victoria has the type of personality that, if you don't say no to her out loud, she thinks it's a yes. (She and Quinny have that in common. Maybe that's why they're friends.)

I sit there and think about her invitation for a moment.

And then I don't say no.

Thirty-nine
Quinny

I can't believe it—today finally got here!

It's the day of our Winter Holiday Assembly, plus our classroom party, which won't be ruined by the new food rules anymore since Principal Ramsey fell for our compromise.

After breakfast, Daddy and I wrap up the coconut snowballs we baked last night in wax paper and put them into a big dish. Then we write a list of the ingredients we used (including fresh eggs from our very own flock of chickens), and tape it to the plate. Everybody who's bringing food to our holiday party has to do that, to prove there are no nuts, and so people with other allergies can stay safe.

It's very, very, extra-very hard to not break into these cookies on the schoolbus, let me tell you. Luckily, I got an A-plus in Schoolbus Studies, so I use all my smarts to leave them alone.

At school, all the learning is canceled this morning! Ms. Bing says we still need a lot of practice before the holiday assembly, so we have an extra double-chorus session instead.

In chorus, we sing "Dreidel Dreidel Dreidel" so many times in a row that it really should be called "Dreidel Dreidel Dreidel Dreidel Dreidel Dreidel."

Then she gives me the wood block and I go up front. I'm so excited because it's time for "Jingle Bells"—one of my favorite songs ever.

I try to catch Hopper's eye to show him my excitement. He's in the back row staring down at his shoes, and he doesn't look up. Neither does Juniper, a couple of kids away from him. Her face tilts down so much that all I see is the zigzag part in her wispy brown hair. The two of them must have the most fascinating shoes in the world.

I don't know anything about Juniper, except what Hopper once told me—that she only pretends to sing. Can she whistle with two fingers? What's her favorite cookie? Is that cool zigzag part in her hair on purpose, or does she just not comb her hair in the mornings? I think about all the things I don't know about that girl.

"Quinny, pay attention, please," says Ms. Bing. "You missed your cue to start banging."

"Oh, sorry!"

I start banging, and keep thinking . . . Ms. Bing doesn't talk to Hopper or Juniper too much. I think maybe our school has some quiet kids who don't get noticed just because they don't bang their personalities out into the world. Hopper is interesting if you know the inside of his personality, but the outside of it is basically just a turtle shell. If I hadn't met him over the summer, when it was just us on our street, would he and I even be friends?

It makes me shiver to imagine not being Hopper's friend.

I think of the report card he made for me.

I remember my *A-plus* in One-of-a-Kindness.

I look down at my wood block. It's shiny and hard, and it makes a wonderful popping crackle every time I hit it, like a horse clomping along the road.

"Ms. Bing, wait." I rush over to her and whisper, "Can I switch with Juniper?"

"Excuse me?"

"Juniper Dunne, in the back. You know, she's been in chorus with me this whole time. I have a feeling she'd be amazing at wood block. Let's give her a chance, shall we?"

Ms. Bing gives me the weirdest look.

"Quinny, we're performing this afternoon—it's too late to change anything."

"Ms. Bing, it's not too late. You're the teacher, it's up to you, but personally I think it's a great idea, because Juniper never gets a turn very much and doesn't even look up from her shoes, and getting picked to bang the wood block could give her a little boost, you know?"

Ms. Bing keeps looking at me like I am a very strange puzzle, and then a sad little smile creeps across her mouth. "Quinny, you're right. It's a lovely idea. Wish I'd thought of it myself."

"That's okay, Ms. Bing, you can still use it

even if you didn't think of it, because ideas should belong to everyone."

Ms. Bing calls Juniper down to the front and asks her if she'd like to play the wood block for "Jingle Bells." Juniper looks at me, like this is some kind of joke, so I say, "It's no joke, Juniper, we were just chatting about how you'd be awesome at the wood block. Here, take it."

Juniper shakes her head.

But I nod my head. I use my *Keep Trying* muscles to convince her, and finally she gives up saying no and lets me hand her the wood block.

Except, it's harder handing that wood block over to Juniper than I thought it would be.

I really do love banging on it.

So now I have to use my *Keep Trying* muscles on myself. And they get kind of sore.

But the look on Juniper's face as she accepts the wood block from me is totally worth it.

Hopper

In chorus, we sing "Dreidel Dreidel Dreidel" so many times that I lose count. Then Ms. Bing makes us practice "Jingle Bells" over and over, too. And I am not laughing all the way, ha ha ha.

Then there's some problem with the wood block, so Quinny switches places with Juniper, and we have to sing it three more times, ugh.

"Jingle Bells" sounds the same when Juniper plays the wood block as when Quinny did.

But it looks a lot different.

It's weird seeing Juniper up front. Weird, but kind of great. Ms. Bing is a pretty good music teacher, but I wonder how chorus would feel if she didn't play favorites so much.

I don't talk at lunch, because I know the rest of the afternoon will be noisy. I need to store up some quiet to get through all the holiday assembly hoopla that's coming up.

At recess, I go over to the Books & Buddies Bench. Jayson is there, reading a comic book. Buck sits on the ground nearby, drawing in the dirt with a stick. Behind the bench, leaning on it, are Juniper and Quinny, reading something about zombies. And nearby, Victoria is alphabetizing the books in the Little Free Library. She also tapes up a flyer to the side of it.

It's the best kind of recess. Nobody bugs me, but I don't feel alone.

At the end, when the bell rings, I see Kaitlin peeking inside that Little Free Library.

She takes a book out and walks away, fast.

I can't see the title of that book, but I see part of the picture on the cover.

And it's of a lady dancing with a cat.

* * *

COME JOIN OUR
NEW BOOK CLUB,
STARTING NEXT WEEK
AT RECESS.

Bookies & sparkling water
will be served. A vote will
be taken to pick our first
book, and everyone's ideas
are welcome. ♡

After recess, it's time for the Winter Holiday Assembly.

I head to the gym with everyone, and brace myself for all the noise and all the people and all the screechy chairs. Principal Ramsey gets up and welcomes us and thanks us for coming to this assembly, like we had any choice. Then Ms. Bing gets up to welcome us, again. Then all the grades take turns doing their chorus songs.

When it's time for the third grade to get up and sing, I'm relieved that I get to stand in the back row. No one ever looks at me back here. All I have to do is wait for the songs to finish, and then I can get off this stage.

I can't wait for this assembly to be over. I can't wait to get home. I want to read with Piper and the chickens, and play chess by myself, and start my new anatomy model. (I used some of my birthday money to buy myself a lung. The cool thing about human lungs is that they're made up of even more parts than ears, including thousands of these tiny air sacs called alveoli that swoosh around the swampy, spongy insides of a lung.)

But once all the grades are done doing their singing, we don't get to leave, because Principal Ramsey gets up and starts talking again.

"Hold up, everyone," he says. "I know we're all excited to get to our classroom parties, but before we dismiss from this incredible Winter Holiday Assembly, we have one last special announcement. Normally I do this kind of thing over the loudspeaker, but this time it felt right to do it here, in front of our entire school community. I'm talking about the STOMP award . . . the Student of the Month Prize. December's award goes to a student who has positively impacted the lives of all of us at WVES, someone whose generosity and thoughtfulness are undeniable."

I shift in my seat. Usually the STOMP winner is an older kid, or someone with a big personality who's on student council or peer leadership, or something like that.

But today is unusual.

Mr. Ramsey looks over to where my class is sitting.

"Today, I'd like to present the Whisper Valley Elementary School STOMP award to Hopper Grey."

Forty-one

Quinny

Wow! Principal Ramsey just called out Hopper's name for STOMP, so I whistle with two fingers to celebrate, which makes the kids next to me jump. I can't believe it, this is the first time I've ever heard Hopper's name come out of an official school microphone.

I'm excited, but the truth is, I'm not too shocked. Hopper really deserves that STOMP award. Everybody's clapping for him now, but he isn't moving. He just sits there, two rows behind me, looking startled. I guess he needs a little boost to go up and get that award.

So I leave my seat.

A few *excuse me's* and *pardon me's* later, I'm standing right by him, close enough to poke his shoulder hello.

Only it's not Hopper I'm poking; this must be the wax-museum version of Hopper. Because that boy is scared stiff.

Forty-two

Hopper

My name makes no sense coming out of Principal Ramsey's mouth.

People are staring and murmuring and clapping.

But I just want to run and hide. I don't belong up there on the stage.

"Hi!"

Quinny's in my row, in front of me, all of a sudden. "Hopper, guess what? You just won STOMP, so let's go get that award, shall we?" She pulls me down the row and up the aisle and onto the stage. My body feels numb except for my wrist, which hurts because she's squeezing it. But I'm glad Quinny grabbed my wrist, not my hand. I don't want to hold hands with her, especially not in front of the whole school.

We get to Principal Ramsey, who looks down at me as he keeps talking to the crowd. He says I helped change the food rules by proposing a smart compromise. He says I made the Friendship Bench a more interesting place to be at recess, and "planted the seed" for the Little Free Library. He says I'm helping a classmate improve at math, and a kindergartner learn to read, by reading to chickens.

Everyone laughs at that. I feel my face burn.

Principal Ramsey says I do a lot, but never toot my own horn. He says my creativity, generosity, and humility are a powerful combination.

This is so weird. No one ever notices me. But now everyone does, all at once.

And it's too much. The sound of everybody clapping crashes into my ears.

Principal Ramsey puts the STOMP medal around my neck. He hands me a paper.

I stare down at it, because anything is better than looking out at all those people.

Piper is terrible at drawing. And she spelled my name wrong, with just one *p*: *Hoper*.

But still, I know I'm never going to throw this picture away, ever.

Forty-three

Quinny

So the other exciting thing that happened today, besides Hopper almost fainting when he got the STOMP award, was that Juniper did a great job on the wood block. (I would have done it a tiny bit better, since I had more practice, but still, she was great.)

And now we are all celebrating at our classroom party!

Cecily brought crunch-in-your-mouth benne wafers and melt-in-your-mouth banana cake for Kwanzaa.

Izzy and Caleb brought sweet latkes, chocolate marshmallow dreidels, and rugelach cookies for Hanukkah.

TJ brought fruit leather that she made herself, just because.

And a bunch of people brought all kinds of magnificent Christmas treats, like strawberry santas, iced gingerbread trees, peppermint bark, muddy reindeer and supermarket sugar cookies. Not to mention my famous coconut snowballs!

There is so much to celebrate I don't even know where to start.

Of course there's a table of strictly healthy, noncookie stuff, too. Like fruit, and veggies and hummus, and blah blah blah. I'll save those veggies for dessert, I think. If I have any room left.

"Sweet." Alex loads his plate with cookies. "Thanks for saving our holiday party, Big Foot."

"Quinny's name isn't Big Foot, so stop calling her that," says Victoria.

"Actually, Hopper is the one who saved this party," I tell everyone. "He invented that new and improved petition for Principal Ramsey, not me."

Hopper turns red, again. He doesn't want to take credit for anything, so I have to shove that credit down his throat. Along with a coconut snowball or two. We walk around the room, making plates for ourselves. I don't want to leave out any of the treats. Every winter holiday deserves respect.

Hmmmm . . . I wonder if anyone is going to eat all that leftover powdered sugar on this empty platter. It's not right to waste food. I swipe a finger along the platter and make a smiley face. Then I dip that sugary finger into my mouth, where it tastes so happy.

The powdered sugar on this platter reminds me of the powdered sugar falling from the sky.

Out the window, I watch it float down onto the sidewalk now.

And then I realize—I AM WATCHING SNOW FALL ON THE SIDEWALK!

I suck in my breath. I go and grab Hopper's arm.

"Hopper Hopper Hopper, look!"

I drag him closer to the window and we stare outside.

Snow changes *everything.*

"Hopper, do you realize what this means? We'll get a snow day tomorrow and go sledding! Do you have snow pants? I have the best sled—I can't wait to show you—it's orange and green and it goes superfast. Daddy got it from the thrift store back in New York. Do you want to sit in the front or the back?"

Hopper looks confused. "I have snow pants," he says.

"Where do you love to go sledding around here? Tell me right this minute!"

"Quinny, it's barely snowing."

"Ooh, there's going to be a blizzard, I just know it!"

"The snow's not even sticking."

"A blizzard and a snow day. There's a really steep hill by Victoria's house, I saw it once, what's that thing called?"

"Mount Roar," roars Alex.

"Are you kidding me? That's a perfect name for a sledding hill!"

I picture it: me and Hopper on my sled, zooming down Mount Roar.

"Yeah, it's pretty lame, except for the Death Drop and Barf Bumps," says Alex.

Is he serious? Death Drop? Barf Bumps? This all sounds too good to be true.

"Hey, Hopper, let's go sledding right after school!"

"Slow down," says Hopper. "Remember, you got hurt skating and swimming."

"But my sprain from skating is all healed and my belly flop from the pool stopped stinging ages ago, so I'm fine to go sledding, I really am! Besides, Hopper, I'm sure it'll only take a few seconds to zoom down that hill—what could go wrong?"

Forty-four

Hopper

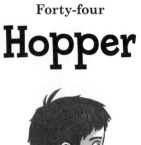

Everything. That's what could go wrong.

It's amazing how Quinny never thinks about that. She's getting carried away now with all her sledding talk. Only a few snowflakes are falling. Yesterday it was so warm that half the kids weren't wearing coats at recess. Last week Alex was still wearing shorts.

"Quinny, don't get your hopes up, it's barely snowing."

"I bet a blizzard is coming. And a snow day. Let's celebrate that blizzard right now!"

She raises her cup of water. (Principal Ramsey said no sugary drinks at the party.)

"Cheers to sledding down Mount Roar, which is the best name for a mountain ever."

"Quinny, it's really just a hill—"

"And cheers to your STOMP award, and to Juniper's wood block—Juniper, get over here, we are doing a cheers! Also, cheers to my almost-a-B in math last week, and the cookies in our tummies, and friends in our hearts, and all the chickens popping out eggs!"

There's no use arguing with Quinny when she gets this excited.

I tap my cup of water against hers. Cheers.

Still, I'm pretty sure there isn't going to be a blizzard.

I turn back to the window and look outside.

The snow is coming down in slow motion, in fat, gentle flakes.

Falling snow makes the world feel calmer.

I could sit here and stare at it forever.

Forty-five

Quinny

Boy, do I love being right!

It snowed a ton, and school the next day *was* really, truly, absolutely canceled.

Now we're about to sled down Mount Roar, which is covered with nine inches of glorious, fluffy, crunchy-powdery brand-new snow.

Mount Roar is the fanciest, highest part of Whisper Valley, and leads down to the valley part, where the rest of the town lives, like me and Hopper. It's not as noisy as it sounds. It's mostly a gentle, pretty hill, but there's one part, all the way to the left by the pine trees, that goes almost straight down, and some older boys made it even steeper by piling snow into a mound at the top.

They really did nickname it the Death Drop. Alex wasn't lying. And on the way down the Death Drop are a couple of Barf Bumps.

None of the parents of the smaller kids are letting them sled down that part of the hill, for some strange reason.

But Mom went back to the car to get dry mittens for Piper, and she left us with Caleb's mom, who is on the phone, so I drag Hopper over to the Death Drop because now is our chance to sneak in some truly exciting fun.

"Hopper, look, that's where all the middle schoolers are going down. I bet no third grader ever went down here . . . let's do it, we'll be legends, let's go for it."

"I don't think that's such a good idea. Your mom will get mad. And, we might die."

"Hopper, I promise we won't die. And look, the hill is so steep, it'll only take two seconds to zoom down it, I promise. We'll be done before Mom even gets back and we'll be together the whole time—don't worry."

Hopper laughs. Which almost never happens. It's such a great sound.

Finally he gets behind me on my sled. He has to grab on to me to keep us together, which feels almost like a hug. A hug that strangles my ribs.

"Ready?" I say.

"Ready. . . . Wait, no—"

Hopper starts to get up, but I scoot us forward to get started before he can run away.

"Yes, you are! Ready, set—"

"No—"

"Go!"

"No, Quinny, I don't think this is such a great ideAAAAAAAAAAAAAAAAA!"

Forty-six

Hopper

I'm going to die, I'm going to die, I'm going to die.

I close my eyes. I cling to Quinny.

This is it. Good-bye, world.

On the other hand . . .

Maybe I won't die just yet.

I hope I don't.

I hope I live to drink some hot chocolate after all this. I guess it's better to hope a good thing will happen than to worry a bad thing will.

What did Piper call me in her drawing, again?

Hoper.

My name is Hopper, the Hoper.

281

Forty-seven

Quinny

Who knew Hopper had that much noise inside him? More noise than Cleo, even.

Zooming straight down the Death Drop is awesome, even though I can't hear so great afterward. I tumble off the sled and shake my head, and hope everything inside it goes back to normal soon. Freeze-y snow fizzes up my nose and tingles inside my boots.

Hopper's plopped sideways in the snow, too. His eyes look all big and buggy. His mouth pops open. His breath comes out huffy-puffy.

"Hopper, are you okay?"

He doesn't answer.

But then he sits up, and his mouth curls into a smile, and one tiny word comes out:

"Again?"